CW01080560

Selling My LAST SUIT

RICHARD PAGE

authorHOUSE®

AuthorHouse™ UK
1663 Liberty Drive
Bloomington, IN 47403 USA
www.authorhouse.co.uk
Phone: 0800 047 8203 (Domestic TFN)
*   +44 1908 723714 (International)*

Published by AuthorHouse 09/26/2019

ISBN: 978-1-7283-9419-0 (sc)
ISBN: 978-1-7283-9420-6 (e)

– CHAPTER –
ONE

1.   Gone were the days when I had a suite of one of a kind, likely from the Buffalo Bill cuts in two pieces. The trousers and the double breasted jacket. Gone were the days on Sunday afternoon going to the Majestic cinema native screen to watch the old western with cops, robbers and like tombstone territory. Pops corns, ice scream and in the dark night belching out the wind from over indulgence of the coco cola I had just drank. The going home with no girls and Elves Presley hits about a "man shook up" blasting out from every radio stations and from the jukeboxes of corner shops up and down the street was not nice for a lonely boy. Streets were ablaze with lonesome songs. At night I listen to the music and the beat and the restless words that have gone through my juvenile scull. Gone are the favoured few that had past the contract test and travel to the United States to work on the farm to become a farm worker. And one could not miss out on "O Coral I am but a fool," Hits of many that were blasting out throughout every states of the union.

2.   Matthew tells me about a man coming to visit the camp that evening and to order my first suit as though he was a Tailor himself. He described the suit as though he was going to wear it to his wedding, but later on I found out that Matthew was already married and a guy he called JG had taken his wife away from him while on his travel. The man name was Buffalo Bill who came to the camp site where we were for a short while. Buffalo Bill holds respect any where he goes by former

farm workers. He was the king of sales and punctuality travelling from the suburb of the Bronx in New York to Wisconsin on time. He was on time and any one misses that time would have to wait a long time after he come and gone. Or even between a few months before he would come again. He would not be visiting for another month or so with the suits the farm workers ordered. No doubt he had contacts within the system that feeds him with details should in case the customer slipped the contract or gone onto another farm in another state.

3.   There were four of the main countries at an early age I wanted to travel although I did not know why. The United States of America, Britain, Russia and Germany. Maybe it was in the tone of their name why it riveted in my memory that when I grew up and have that chance I would like to travel. It may be coincidence of the first one on the list had come true and when the chance comes, it was with trepidation. But it had to be taken, because it was in the dream to travel to these countries one day. The first was the United States of America where the older travellers had taken me under their arms and teaches me to collect the incentive and to spend it in the future even when they were no more.

4.   When he came to visit and introduced to the new Afflicts he normal brings some sort of entertainer to entertain while he does his sale line. Once he brought a native with one of the largest boa constrictor snake skin may have been found in southern United States. The glee about Buffalo Bill was immensely popular bought

on by his reasonable reason to sell diverse material and convincingly shows them how it would fit the farm worker for the women they leave behind in their native country. He placed the man in the suit and then shows him the metaphors of walking to the cinema in the distant future with a girl, and how she would view him as god with this suit on. It did not matter whether it was a wife a sweetheart, girlfriend or just a girl who has eyes for a returning traveller.

5.   I was now introducing to Buffalo as a man-boy of nineteen still a juvenile. I could not vote then nor married unless I seek permission to do so and hardly would I have wanted to married so early when life was budding comfortable and just being away from mother and sister's control and careful care. I need this time to make changes for myself and make some mistakes thrown in as well until I become man at twenty one years old. I had another two to three years to go. The first thing that I wanted was a fragrance Buffalo calls "young lover." It smells at first awful but after a little while the armour was nicely putted and lasted for a long while on the clothes we wear. I had six weeks before turning nineteen years old. Nineteen, twenty and twenty one, counting down the days left. I could hide to court a girl but reserve to go public would be a matter of talking to my mother and guardian.

6.   Buffalo Bill selling pitch when I was examining the demo package that he bought for customer to look and chose their pattern from, goes like this, 'You don't

have to wear it. You can sleep in it. You can play in it, crop all week in it and wear it to your work all day. Wear it to the cinema with your girl Saturday night and then go to church Sunday morning in it. It never creases nor loses its seams. It works like this-it's a pyjama a casual dress and high class suit to dress in, goes to the dance and never ever pick up bits. It's not a suit to wear, it's a suit to live in.' He got style and any man heard Buffalo pitch and did not do business with him would be inconsiderate.

7.   Matthew taken me through the sample material and put on his animation style when doing so, behaving as throughout how the cut would obviously fitted around me. My first suit from Uncle Sam was being considered. However, I could not afford it right away, it was eighty dollars Buffalo wanted for the cut. It was a black cut, two pieces double breasted jacket with its tail ended at the tip of my middle finger. The trousers was a baggy straight cut tapered off to a small ending with the cuffs turned over to blended with the straight seam just lengthening enough to the top of the black loafer with the socks formed a wavy curls as with the girl walking beside me.

8.   Anything less than that, Matthew would have gone bizarre. I know when he was not himself. He lighted the full strength capstan cigarettes and stumps them out quite quickly, one after the other. There was no none smoking area and he could smoke in bed if he wishes to, which he had done too. Matthew was small in stature

and fair complexion man he would sulks a lot when things were not going his way. Some of the Afflicts called him 'cry baby.' Afflicts was the new name given to the new comers by the older farm workers who for a while dominated and collar the scene. We were not coined as immigrants and never had that status encode upon us by anyone.

9.   Buffalo asking for fifty per cent as deposit for the cut and Matthew take measurement for dark tweed material while the other goes for less flashy style I was encouraged to go for the top, since it was probable my first and could be my last suit from Uncle Sam. Matthew offered me the deposit of forty dollars and told me that I could pay him back at any time before we were sent to other camps and parted.

10.   Now I got a suite ordered and much more becomes a debtor to which seem to be trigger off by far an encouragement from an older man. I now owed forty dollars of Matthews's money and another forty which must be paid when the suit is delivered a month's time. Supposed, I pondered, Buffalo did not return then it would be of little benefit to me I would still half owed on the suit I did not possess as yet.

As far as the law was concern, I was still a youth then and should not allow to barrowed from any critical lender. I mean an official lender; because I was still under age and anywhere I had gone throughout the western world I would still be class as under age juvenile. Even more atrocious name of being calls juvenile delinquent, and green behind the ears. By all means I could not discourage him from lending me the forty dollars, but then I could have argued that he influenced me to barrowed his money. I had been to hold a meeting with myself about the reason and reasonableness of my critical analysis of the situation I found myself in. My mother tuition came into play as part of my memory growing up. She would certainly refer to my spending another man's money has being 'long eyed.' But since I am now travelling I surely was allowed to make mistakes while I don't go too far with my barrowing. Not too far but not near enough and my mind would tumbling over my first big debt.

- CHAPTER -
TWO

11.   Matthew was my friend an older man that has chosen me to be his best friend at that particular time. Was it that he could not find friends amongst his age to be friendly with instead of me? It could be a complimented scenario, but then I argued that it could not be as he has told me that his first son was about my age. The child's mother would not allow him near to his son for him to be his rightful father. This Matthew had begrudged the man who now his son calls 'daddy.' His son was given a name also which he had detested, but he walked out on the woman when she becomes pregnant.

12.   "If I had my girl and she becomes pregnant, with my child I would not leave her until I die." I told him. "You're too young to understand women." He replied. "But, one day you will, and that day isn't far off." This was reassuring to me, that an older man could be openly acknowledged that I was on my way to being a man. He had plugged me my first full strength capstan cigarettes during the conversation that evening and since he had moved his belongings to the spear bunk bed on the lower deck we smoked in bed, but I had a frightful coughing that arises some of the occupants at night. To this day I could not tell how it was that my grandmother found out that we were smoking her pipe tobacco. So she locked it away, so it must be our coughing that carries the tell tale.

13.   From back home we use to call the older people Mr or Misses as part of the honour and as for obedience and respect to the older folks. Anything less would

bring immediate retribution. So being an older man I had to give Matthew his honour as being an older person and now that I am on my way to becoming a man myself. Probably when I got back home someone younger might shows me little respect also. That week I picked up one hundred and thirty two dollars beside the extraction of ten percent for the McDonald security insurance savers account for back home.

14.   They had given us five dollars before the four propeller airplane touches down at Illinois air base travelling from Palisados air port Jamaica. When we arrive it had not seem much and for that matter never understand the exchange so I could not equate five dollars from five pounds sterling. Anyway it was not to allow us in Uncle Sam's country broke as most of us were. It was not long though before I cipher out the exchange and found that it was worth less than three quid in British money. Most youngster of my age never seen nor held in their hands a five dollar bill much more five pounds sterling in paper note.

15.   Working out the money I had make it my first and foremost duty as I go along with Matthew guidance and what he had told me to look out for. He had kindly shows me how they worked it out from their side and it was my duty to cipher it out from my side before and after the deduction. Any discrepancy he would go with me to sort my more or less payment, particularly the less payment side. However, a couple of weeks past when Matthew began to compare my payments against

his. He requested to see my payslip as he guesses they were paying him less than they were paying me.

16.   Matthew had now gone back on his word, though, because he was now asking for the things he had council me strongly not to do. Not to show anyone my payslips. He had told me stories about the "bad minded ones and the crooked." After seeing the pay slips he had went into a sulk, but he told me that I would be going home soon and his sulk I would not be travelling with him for very long. I was earning twice as much and for that they were drawing just the same percentages for the fair of eighty four dollars for the company to charter us to the farm that was eighty four dollars inclusive plus the five dollars they had given us when we enter the United States. The equal of my compound debt at the time was over a hundred dollars with that of Matthew's forty dollars.

17.   "If you completely pay off the money within a year they're going to send you back home soon after you finish pay it off." Matthew told me. "I know you're able and young, but if you could hold back for another year." "How do I do that? I asked. "If you owe Uncle Sam money they won't send you home owing them money. So slow down. I don't work hard even to pay my keeps much more to start paying the fair." "Is there anything wrong with that?" "No, only that another year you could earn a few more dollars in your saving and still remain in Uncle Sam's country." CC was listening. He was standing close by over hearing the conversation

within me and Matthew. He was an older man too, but not as old as Matthew were. "We older man is to show these afflicted youth the method we use to stay here." CC commented. "You don't want to go back so early on the rock, do you?"

- CHAPTER -
THREE

18.   As long as I remain in the company of these men being the youngest for several months I would learn then that things on the surfaces were not as they seems. I thought that I had picked up things that might have carried me through life and many of the time it does. I learn in a different ways to manipulate my surroundings and further gained respect from the older men to the young ones. My time with them deeply ingrained and trains me in almost every aspect of live and stretches my tentacles in the combat for life without controlling my ability to function as a youth.

19.   The weekend a months later the suit arrived and Buffalo called me to try on my new black suit. Matthew were looking on with CC and the others as I putted my right hand and then Buffalo took the left hand and pull the jacket over and see that I was dressed. They were dressing me as though I was going to my own funeral. Matthew came over and rubbed his hands over the shoulder of cloth, and asked the other groups to put their hands for a clap over owning my first Uncle Sam cut. I had never owned anything before that was purchase with my own money. This was the first big money I was allowed to spend freely and eighty dollars all at once was much.

20.   This was a good cut and feels so good and comfortable. Matthew did not overlook anything an all that when I stretch down my hands fully it was to be at the tip of the middle finger. He was one who helped to give praise and seem that the man was righteous too. By

the way my name is Pcagd pronounce Page, my name has brought on many raised eye brows since like myself it was given to me by my father who died soon after. It is alright until when I am signing document whether legal or not. On the point of which page this one or that one I would say on the other one.

21.   Now that we have got over the spelling of my name and the other rig-ma-rows I would not forget my name. Matthew and I had entered into relationship that was interested for me, and being with him it was like being with a father figure. Girls would often be mention in our conversation but his main concern was also about my welfare and about the dollars I earned. He show and tells me how I might save and be better off and since I was an Afflict like many of us and he had travelled and previously experience he was in a better position to be my sort of an unpaid councillor.

22.   We spent five weeks at the Fox lake establishment of the Green Giant company in Wisconsin USA gathering the corn crops. The pay was fortnightly and so Matthew was on hand to direct how to spend and holding back for me to survive until the next pay cheque. He was youth too, and may realised that I would spend the money all of it straight away. He was aware about something else; that we could separate at a moment notice and sent to different farmers allowing only a day or even shorter. This was revealing, because it was never a guarantee that our friends that were made during this kind of travel would sustained.

23.   Sometimes they may be sent hundreds of miles away and very seldom any contact can be made. Being aware of this Matthew would pack and being on full alert even before he was told so. He had requested me to do the same, as being delay could lose an opportunity. Farmers are patient in one way but in another way they are not. This was especially true when it's time for their crops to be gathered in. My cut now meant that small bag that I travelled with becomes too small and my new cut would have to be carefully stored and could not fit in the small case. Matthew encourage that I should not purchase a suitcase yet and so early on in my first travel. So I did not do so to hold my new outfit.

24.   All sort of sale men would visited the camp at where we were staying, and anything could be purchase from them on order. We need not going to the city Milwaukie to purchase anything since they brought the necessary stuff which by then the salesmen must have known and developed a method what farm workers mostly buy. This they might have been doing since nineteen forty four when the Americans negotiate with the British to send men to help with their crops from the Caribbean. Many farms were then own or partly own by the British or mixed American and British family anyway we have learned.

25.   So in effect we were working in line with an agreement that the Caribbean men would be working to feed the much needed depleted world stocks, and Brittan would be greatly benefitted. Our Government

SELLING MY LAST SUIT

never told us how it was done and beside I was too young to know much about anything. It was only since I was now in my six weeks away from home that I had quickly becoming aware of the world at large. History was something told on the black board and meant nothing to me at that age. The flag waving and all the regalia was not to impress me at that age neither would be my colleagues. The Marco Polo, Venice the Fareast and the Middle East the North Pole and South Pole were only on a map and may not have even belonging to this globe at all.

26.   Getting my new outfit was an eye opener and bought with my own earnings and being a guest in one of the most prosperous and huge country of the world. Remembering what my navigator asked me to do if he gave me the chance to enter the USA. Before he stamps his part of the first hurdle "Page, if I give you the chance to enter the United States of America will you promise to behave yourself?" I replied "yes." It seems that he had put faith in my youthfulness that many did not at the time, and that I would behave. Only thing that stood in the way was whether I could give a good blood test for the completing and overcome the first of many hurdles.

27.   Recalling my adopted parents wishes me to learn to be a motor mechanical to servicing large and small vehicle. The first day the second and up to six weeks I was still scraping and polishing out the huge back axle white bearing housing without let up from the old boss man. When I taught I completed the task he would

inspect and find and pointed out where I missed out and rejected the work. Then he would tell me that I had to get it right before he could move me on to other things. This other things had given me hope that somewhere in his mind that Mr C. Jiles was thinking about me and sooner rather than later he would have to do something about applying his conscience. I had the tenacity to be persistence which he may not like very well. It might annoy the old brute too; soon he relented and starts to speak to me in a more tuneable voice of encouragement.

28.   The other boys who were there before I joined the school told me that Mr Jiles was a hard man to please and they had had the same done to them. So while a think he was picking at me I had overcome the behavioural problems, knowing that he had a clever way of seeing his student through, through disciplining them from their earliest days with him. This was, so that later he could rely on them for efficiency in their work and what they do would be next to perfection and pleases him.

29.   In the normal weekly instructions he regularly mention about vehicle malicious overhaul behaviour and when customer take their vehicle to us for repair though it may be costly it must be done to our best abilities. "Your abilities to faction without shortcut or malpractice are important to the safety of the vehicle and the occupant." This was Mr C Jiles' motto. So when the question was put to me by the examiner whether I would behave myself when I get into the United States

of America I had no problem with the answer and to reply in the affirmative.

30.   On growing up I had taken many pointers from older people and also the eldest of my colleagues and although Matthew was not too older than I was, but could be my father. His behaviour toward me shows that he too had had some discipline from others and a far off experience. He had travelled the farmer contract two or three times previously and he had becomes wise from being my free hand councillor. Those who he notice that seems to be turbulent he asked me to avoid. We had finish reaping the corn at the Green Giant outlet and they were now assessing where they would dispatches us to and which farmer crops were ready for picking.

31.   If the crops were not yet ready we would remain at Foxlake camp until such time as the other farms where we assign to crops were ready for us. In that time we would be eating and occupying the Green Giant facilities which had to pay for by somebody. And that somebody would be us on credit. Some workers had come in from the Rosendale camp at the Foxlake accommodation for dispatch as well to other states wherever their crops were ready to pick.

32.   Some would be going to Michigan to pick cherries, to Ohio to pick apple to Florida to cut cane and pick orange and grapefruits. Others would be going to New York for picking apples, to Arkansas to pick Cotton and to other states included. The radio stations would be

pumping out the new hits and especially the new release "o coral I am but a fool," and others. With forty or more radio in the camp and everybody wanted to hear their own hits, turn on their radio and no matter if the other person on the top or the bottom bunk, that was how it goes. Particularly if that was his first radio he owned and purchase with his hard earning dollars.

- CHAPTER -
FOUR

33.   "When one waiting at camp for transfer anything after the farmer finishes with you, you've got to pay for it." Matthew told me and those of the new afflicted visitors. Some of us were chosen from source to go to special farmers. The young and agile he male that could move fast and faster still, and having the strength of a agile gazelle for the next day work, and work as hard as the day before and even harder. The farm worker on the northern side faces obstacles for working hard to get in the crops. Not too hard though that he would put himself out of work and beside where pay per keeps was in force.

34.   Three days later the representative for some of the farmers came along and twenty of us were chosen to go to Ohio a place just outside Youngstown to work on the Faunally apple orchard. This orchard was special, full of luscious apples and dollars spinning per boxes. It seems that he had had farm workers before since we were well received, his wife were an English woman and very kind. We had our own cook that now becomes part of our travelling itinerary to feed all twenty of us. He had the privileged of contacting owner's wife for anything that was short or missing.

35.   Apples were in abundant and Mr Faunally promised that he would pay us incentives if we were to gathering the crop before the winter months. With that in mind, we surmised that some farm worker may let him down in the past and some of his crop was not gather in before the winter season and he had lost a

good many that should have been gathered in. So from the start we had was to work late in the evening and because the farm was secluded and not so near the town centre we only could visit on weekends, but this was restricted to no visits at all until the crops were completely reaped.

36. I had left Matthew at Foxlake Wisconsin, but the cook feeds us with the news that he too came to Ohio a little way from us and that one weekends we could hire a vehicle to go and see these fellows. Matthew had mention several times about being a comrade that I did not understand and he never talked much about it in my presence. It was CC that had asked me what has happen to my communist friend, although he did not elaborate much he had given me something to think about. Whether we would be allowed to consult a dictionary, although the cook had one I see no need was to look it up, since the older men looked on as being truthful.

37. Both the older men at the camp and those travel with us I notice would avoid Matthew, and an occasion when they were talking and he comes along they would walk away or scattered. At the garage Mr Jiles told his student and I being a part of it: ""I can't sell nor give none of you experience, but you'll soon learn as you goes along in life. You'll have to pick your friends. Some will pick you and others will reject you for no apparent reason. Most of your friends will want to be your friends anyway. Those who reject you will reject you no matter how hard you've tried. They just don't

want to be with you, in your company nor want you be in there's. This is called toleration you tolerate the rejection and go about your own business, as others tolerate you."

38. "You'll have close friends and distant friends, short terms friends and long terms friends. Those who want to be with you and those who have seldom hear from or will ever see again. Some or family friends and others or so-called friends. You'll have social friends and some will never be your friend at all. Like the pretentious friends and varied friends depending on the colour of the friendship, but you're going to have friends no matter how low down life's travel you're going to meet them all."

39. I had just gone nineteen years old and on this first of my voyage I learned within a few weeks that folks will teach and say something that remain and service to you throughout life travel. And as my folks used to say: "you're never too old to learn." It was the Sunday following our travel to Ohio that Matthew with a few other of the men had make their visits to the Faunally's orchard. We heard when the vehicle pulled up at the camp door, and I had been the nearest of the windows and saw a bottle green taxi pulled up with the five men from the Foxlake compound started to unload.

40. I could recognise Matthew and the others unloading from the car. The cook immediately went out to meet them after I shouted that it was the men

from Foxlake. I notice that the cook had stop them from entering the camp, but also went to the Faunally's packing works which was working not far away, and Mr Faunally himself had come over and speak to the men. I could not hear what the exchange was but they were reloading up the vehicle. I unhesitatingly went out following what I saw followed by CC and Britain another young man a little older than I was.

41.   The taxi engine did not switches of and the Buick engine was still humming and was ticking over beautifully when the men commence to reload. Matthew was the last to re-entered the car so I grabbed the handshake and before we waved him off he inquire about me and my new UNCLE SAM garment. Just then and after that commotion and I went back in the camp I looked up my new outfit. It was single bed and at the head of the bed the suit was hanging and the cloth feel that I could living in it as the day Buffalo had fitted the suit on me. Britain had inquired whether I would sell the suit to him but I at once rejected the notion and told him so.

42.   I wanted then to know from the cook what has gone on and why the car had turn round with its passengers and leave, now that I was a man surely I should asked man to man question: "they did not inform neither the Faunally nor their owner that they were coming over here," he told us. "Are they coming back then later?" "No, I don't think so, for today." "Matthew, should've known that?" "He probably knows that you can't go

from one farm to the other without consulting with the other farm you're visiting. Many of it is safety guard and some of these boys will want to slip the contract and caused a lot of problem and disruption to us who're stable."

43.   Mathew shouted as the Buick slides away, "Remember, when you can, get a white shirt, you must, It matches the black suit. And some cuffs to go with it!" CC commented that because Matthew was a communist nobody would pay any mind to what he was saying, even if it's true what he said. The built in complaining procedures was through a Liaison Officers appointed by both government for their subjects. Then for us we would be subject as from the empire rules subjects of the Crown of the United Kingdom and Colonies.

- CHAPTER -
FIVE

44.   So instead of appointments of different country appointees for compliant procedures it would be one appointment that satisfied the whole criteria. All the countries in the Caribbean have come under these subjective procedures. The appointed officer would be centrally located. Any disputes would be quickly dwelt with and sorted out. Although it was before the word coined 24/7 it was in operation and use long before the legitimate of this hyphen word in use as it is today. The officers had to be, on hand just in case something happens that was serious during the nights to one or more of the farm workers. It also could be triggered by a complaint about another screening off the lower limbs of the apples from the row that was another.

45.   The cook had been a source for information and like a bird he would sings song of what he heard from the grapevine and because he feeds us he probably wanted us to have his confidence. The cook must share his priority. No swings to the other side more than to the men he feeds on the right to that side. He had to be on the sides of the Faunally's and our side and also satisfied his master Her Majesty the Queen of England. Whether he knows it or not, that was how he had to be split the bunch of his legions and right behaviour. He could shows no partially in any way to any of her Caribbean subjects. The liaison Officer appointed would adopted that stance as well as part of the glue that bond our small nation to be one.

46.   He was in very peculiar situation, any upset from any of the party would land him in trouble, but he knows his way around this circle, of being a diplomat in the job for a long time. Because it was a Sunday morning many of us boys would probably be at church or walk about in our district of the country not much to do. Since Sundays were class as a day of rest and that what we were doing at camp on this day of rest. And shallow as it may sound today that's how it was in small community. The city was always a busy place to be for Sundays and for that matter for all the days.

47.   The cook had ask to avoid debating politics and religion as this has caused many grieve that he had seen. Because we are now a small community of twenty one individuals living together. CC commented that at the big camps we could do almost anything, but he agrees that these two subjects should be avoided if at all possible. Britain would not have it, and even to discuss these aggregate would cause the same effect that the cook suggest to avoid. These were the two things brought on lively exchange and we believe it was coming from higher authority and De-Costa suggested that there was a spy amongst us, referring to the cook. But he denied being a spy and refers to his long time serving the community of farm workers.

48.   The car loads of visitors by now got back to their camp, since it was not far distant they had to travel to their destination and they too might be having the same discussion. Both cook know each other from what our

cook had said in the past about Matthews and the others cook. I took the 'stand and see stance,' since I could not understand clearly why the men travel to see us and they could not, because an inbuilt restrictions that would never allow the men to say simple 'hello' regardless.

49. We come a long way since our voyage to experience and growing up too that combine to be in the form of a farm worker. The subject was brought up again on the following Monday when the liaison officer arrived to introduce himself to us. He brought up the subject of what he heard about the next camp visits. It was just after lunch when he came to our camp. Being naive about anything and of everything there were our questions mostly from the Afflicts, about why these men did not allowed staying with us for a little while longer?

50. Of course this was explain with some unexpected turns of events that we had never considered, and would not understood unless someone like the Liaison officers explained. He had pictorially pictured scenarios that even the cook seems to have missed. We understood that anywhere we go we would be watched and any stray away from the farmer's property on our own could bring repercussion. It even could result in our returning home, that we did not want to do, and were restricted in being for that farm alone until such time as when we would be safely handed over to another farmer and becomes a temporary property of that farmer who took us on.

51.   And even at source had we been told this about the contract we would have still gone on with it, because of the incentive of the voyage. We did not sign any contract as such, but as long as one was willing to go through with the test, it was like this an unsigned agreement. Because it is called the 'the contract.' I can recall Matthew arrant about the 'who that has sign the contract,' although he was in a better position than us, because he went on this voyaged on contract before.

52.   In forgoing taught we were likely sold to the highest bidder, probably like on the stock market around the world and at Wall Street too. We were now became commodities and our freedom were curtail to the point of having none. We were allowed to roam on the range and pasturage but not venture outside of the boundaries being the stipulate restriction zone. Any visits would become known to the owner of the farm that the intended visits to be made, and if he wants to turn down that visits it was his privileged to do so. He was answered to the letter of the contract and accordingly to the letter.

53.   But, we have not seen nor read the contract and nobody except the Liaison Officer who waving a few clips sheets of paper when we had asked about the contract and what it meant for us especially us being the Afflicts and naive. Anyway, he pointed out a few things that we should not do as stipulation such as, 'no women visitors allowed, not to try to burn the place down and not to fight and any disputes to let the cook

be aware of it and he would come and sort things out as quick as possible.' Wiley shouts that "it restricted our enjoyment since we can't bring women in there could be a bit of fighting. This would release some of the pent up energy, because we were mostly young men need a woman love to calm us down. Too many bulls, boars or stud in one pen could trigger an eruption."

— CHAPTER —
SIX

54.   "Six, seven, eight weeks since we," he continued, "we haven't seen a woman near 'cept on the TV." "That's all you boy's problems?" he asked. We all replied and confirm that it was our biggest problem. "A pen with all boars will cause temper to rise, and in this little place it will soon be smell like boars pen. We've just come along, but it could be a problem for the near future. We're not nuns." Confirming that Wiley had a fair and valid point, the liaison officer agreed to look into it. But he delayed in doing according the older ones believe it would be.

55.   The liaison officer left with a promised to, 'see what he can do,' fully, understand that on each or most of the men the shortage of women around would be a problem for both young and older stud alike. At the driving and mechanical school Mr Jiles told us about the oil filtration modulators and what was its duty. "On occasion," he continues, "some small particles, such as a grain of sand will passes through to the engine and score the pistons and the housing too. This is big problems, because the whole thing has to be removed and re-bore or scraps the entire engine entirely."

56.   At my ongoing age I was learning to siphon with the inbuilt filtration I had. Some I would rejected outright, others would be put aside for later use, even for years ahead. Those that were not appropriate and those that were not would be stored somewhere until a better and useful time to use it or them. I had gathered to myself whole hosts of instructors outside the immediate

family, and it does not seem any wanted to be that grain of sand according to the engine requirement.

57.   The liaison officers had gone and although it was late in the afternoon we would endeavour to get in some apples before night fall. There were lively discussion follows and continued for some time yet outside and inside the camp. Back at camp Britain reminded us that the cook sat with the liaison officer and make little comment then he turn to me and asked of my opinion. "On what?" I asked. "Let's listen to what the older one or the more experience one said." "It's a sort of a prison," Britain commented.

58.   The cook commented that "I've been with various groups around the states and whilst there were other problems, mostly were women. So he knows and very much aware of the sort of things. He was from Leesburg to Okeelanta and from Mims to Michigan. He's been widely travel and if he hadn't got your interest at heart then he would be out of that job a long time, especially at sugar. Sugar people," he continued, "wouldn't be so kind to him, to let him be around for so long. He was at Foxlake too, while you were there."

59.   I asked, "If he was the only one about?" "No!" the cook answered, several of them about." "You know any other, beside this one?" "A few." One of my sisters consistently told me that I was dribble, and mother used to jump in to stop the fight from commencing. Then it would be market day when she would not be there to put

in, so I had to defend myself and so I did when she was not on spot. Sometime the sisters call in reinforcement to handle the situation. It was suspicious when two or three girls from school that congregate, I consider to be unfriendly suddenly appear on Saturday morning when moms gone on to market comes to visit and being extremely friendly and wanted to get close to me.

60.   In camp there was none of that instrument or confidence built up to calm the younger men. In the army there were all sort of ranks to keep immediate control and restore order quickly, so it must be from source it was inbuilt in the mechanism about the selection of the men chooses to go on the venture. They must be, were watching us from the time of selection to the time when we aboard the aircraft and beyond. Because, although some had passed the first hurdle, it was then another twenty seven method that were put in place and applied before ones get to the aircraft and sat down.

61.   Many were turned away for failing one thing or the other, and before we went back home and to return we had been warned to keep away from prostitutes. The next day when the last method to applied being the testing of the pennies many were found to be dribbling and no longer would be accepted for the venture. Even those who accepted previous venture and their behaviour were questionable, and get onto the aircraft on this trip would be quickly escorted off and taken away. They were recruiting only amiable men of agile and good characters.

62.   I was one now of amiable and had selected and seduced by the incentive, but the reminder of my sister insistence of me being a dribble when I removed onions from my meals because I did not like onions to eat, I did not push home my point. Probably that was why she picked this word as part of my reference and to refer it to me. We had dinner that evening and had a shower and went to bed following the discussion a day being and a day wiser.

- CHAPTER -
SEVEN

63.   A few days later when we went for lunch the cook told us that he received a call from the other camp, to say that they were getting on fine and asked about us and how we were fairing. There was no telephone connection in the camp building, but the cook only could use the communication in the washing and packing factory. This was my big world where Columbus, Marco polo, Walter Raleigh I just entered with buffalo bill suit staring and watching over my persons. I may have missed the historical documentation that says what age they were when they gone on their first break to go to sea or the Wright Brothers developing and learned to fly.

64.   Now I did not bother about the ages of these historical men, and although I had respect for these men they did not leave any information for me personally to follow their footsteps. Even if they did so, I may not have had the same chance to do what they have done, because of limited access and opportunity and not even my father had stayed around long enough that I could grasp some of his input. The ease that I adapted of Matthew and other older men that would be my learning and teaching skills that would carry me through as I go along.

65.   The supervisor that would take us to the field each day too was a lot older than I was. He seem fair enough and how he would selected the picker was by taking twenty tickets and gave us each the first number of the tickets from the pads and then juggle them up and drop

them on the commencement of each rows of the apple orchard. The first to finish his row would start off again at the next row that was not allocated. After he allocated the rows and the men started off he would fetch boxes from the packing factory and also distributes them on each rows.

66. Some morning it was heavily frosted and reminded us sharply that we were in North America that commences to get cold in September. That contract and the incentive were to reap the Lewis's entire crop before the season closes. We had to work sometimes late in the evenings while the sun was out and all for that the men were concern the lack of women about and often some would go off to bed grumbling about the matter loudly so that all could hear. "No use has money in your pocket and can't spend and have fun with women." Would be drowned in the lingering drowsiness took over before whispering off to sleep.

67. The cook fumingly reported that some of the men were having sex with their bed and that statement would not be far from the truth. He was the one to unload and make the beds all the time, so he must knows about what was going on. Some suggested that about the cook, that he never did voiced any opinion about women and some say that women were coming in while we were out working during the day. Britain and I suspected that a few times Wiley and Brown suddenly becomes heavily with headache and sick so badly that the supervisor had to take them back to camp.

68.   This was to spy out the cook to see if he was sneaking in any female while we were out and in the field. Two or three time weekly he would go to Cleveland to shop for groceries and cigarettes and other stuff. Sometimes for quick replacement he would go to Youngstown that was a nearer town. There he may be popping into some brothel or the other to get his kicks this was one of the suggestion and one of the things to be investigated that I hear about going through the camp.

69.   Then if this was the case I consider about our warning to 'keep away from the prostitute fraternity,' after we had gone through the test would not be keeping in line with the message. There would be brazing remarks regarding the cook's comfortableness outside the feelings of the majority. I was consistently keeping my ears to the ground listening for majority opinions that were far fetch and if any to keep away from them. Opinions were flying about diversely as they could be and with some strange ones, much to passes time on and coloured with descriptive analogical wordings.

70.   I had taken myself out of mechanical school without indenture to become a farm worker, so I had to consider the implication regarding my future, and this was it. The future was here with its incentive but subjected to the present what I can learn and obtain to serve that future. The incentive was present but could end by and dependant only on my behaviour even by the action of others which continued to rang out about Mr

C Jiles and would he have me back if I failed in my first travel. My whole future were now pined on behaviour and not on what I can do, or was about my experience, because I had none or very little on the world stages.

71.   Even Useless Ulysses may have had a better chance than I would have been if I failed. When I got my selection card and mention it Mr Jiles took me on his line of reason and mention that failure had never crosses his mind when he attended mechanical engineering croft. Those whom he had selected he had no doubt about their ability to function within the motor trade. "When you've passed out and get that indenture paper, you'll able to command what you want from your employer or you can go on the repair by your own self."

72.   He continued and pointed his index to his head, "if you don't have it, you'll always be subjected to someone. Without a trade you've nothing to offer. There or going to be bad ones and good ones. Having a trade you can walk away from the bad ones, seek another employee or sets up your own business. You could hit failure by the crops, not just by other human."

73.   "You may never have this chance again to travel until you grow up and working, but you've got to think about this," he said, "your trade or your travel. Some gone over to the states and only spend a couple of months and then they're back almost without anything. Go without saying." After that talk with Mr Jiles I had to wait for the call up for over three months bringing

me back now since all that to twenty one weeks in all. "Some return with almost nothing." These words commence to have a bearing as I pondered over the black suit I had, hanging over my bed that white shirt sticking out as though it itself had been to church. It was Matthew's idea and advice that encourage me to purchase suits and white shirt.

74. I had a few dollars in my little suitcase but not enough to operate anything worthwhile back home. I did not told my mother what I was doing and also my adopted parents until I wrote to them and told them that I was now in the United State of America and about my travel. My poor mother, when she got the letter I could see, meteorically her now crying tears dropping out of her eyes, tip, tip when she open the letter and saw the ten dollars I send for her. This was the most she ever had from me and the first. Ten shillings or ten dollars would have confused her about the exchange rates.

- CHAPTER -
EIGHT

75.   It would be a long time for her to get any money from staying on at the mechanical school I was sent at sixteen and half years old, and getting little money for my effort that I had put into it. A pound here and pound there extra for plainly my operation. It would be a long time before I had anything spare to send or give her. With the few dollars I sent for her making me felt justify with my action and unquestionable being agreeable to any reasonable reason. In kind of way I was siphoning off her disappointment of not seeing me passes out of mechanical school with a few dollars. She hopes that I would carry on with the trade.

76.   I know that some of the men at camp were playing up and mostly caused by the lack of female around and the temptation of gone into town to picked up any prostitute they could lay their hands on without the farmer know about it. With a sort of covert operation that could failed, and moreover may jeopardise the whole of the Faunally's crop if caught. This might be why he was offering incentives, because the men previously or some other time did so and were caught off the camp perimeter and sent home.

77.   The perplexing situation I had was that most of the men were far older except Britain who was a few months older. I was the youngest of these men and very seldom they would be listening to me and also being I was the new arrival that means it was three of us in the camp being Afflicts. The downside of all this was that both Britain and I already glean and agree that

48

there was a plan and retrospectively about my almost improbability going back home without I could pay my way and viable trade to rely on. So many factors there were and very little experience to remedy the situation. All now depend upon the liaison officer action, whether he would hurry up the 'leave it with me and I'll see what I can do,' that needed immediate positive allocation.

78.   I was aware about myself and not to let anyone prey on me. A deep analysis of the environment I find myself in would be enough to drive the regrettable crazy on these account that I could not go back now. It was too late; Jiles by now may replace me position at the mechanical school. Mother and my adopted may well concluded that I was a failure. I was now contemplating the envious and the not so envious position I held. None would have been reversible because they were ongoing some at once and others would be spontaneous.

79.   Suppose the men did not play up but something else started to go wrong and the big Uncle Sam could not afford us and send us all back home? Or supposed they started to play up and go to town unknown by the Lewis's and they were caught? I had eleven weeks of growing up and the evolving of the brain to consider the possibility was now endless making decisions. Certainly, I was not going to be preyed on, but by then I learned a few swears words too with vocal to impress fear. Matthew taught me a few mixture of swear words like the F words with the off joined on it, like the P off too.

80. Though I used to use them back home it was not on the older folks but to my colleagues, and friends. Now I could officially used them without holding back, although I could not vote nor taken seriously being still a juvenile. Had my mother could hear me she would wonder if I had gone to being a stinker, as she kindly refers to men who swears. Then after using them I would go back to having a repentant attitude and promised that I would never, never again, but this was my new freedom to exercise my lungs regularly.

81. At night when I woke up I would regurgitated on what I had been thinking while tearing apples from their mother's limb and branches. There being no guidance, not even a camp commander to respect but seem that all would be rely on high behaviour because of the incentive offered and the possibilities of further and even more at the end of a contract completed successfully. The others from the nearby farm still out there willing to come to look for us, and we would too, but from the rebottle of the first try we better not take the chance to go.

82. Two, three weeks had gone and no reply on the female side of inquiries comes in and other suggestion were now making and footing the headlines within our own news gathering media. We long for a reply, and since it was the body immediate requirement and if not remedy the liquid quickly it would gone on to waste. It would continue so for a long time renewing itself and making demands on its occupants so long as in the predicament continue. The point was of the

liaison officer was being neglectful about his duty and promise, only male gender that did not sigh about lack of female on site was the cook.

83.   Had he been voiced his concern and throw a little weight behind us it may or would clarify already, but he was from different species and have no feelings regard women folks. That was the suggestion by some of the men. Brown, CC and Wiley make regular spot check at camp during the day but they had reported nothing unusually was going on. Also Edgar, Barton and Lewis would pop in to use the toilet facilities. John, Thompson and Bruce make occasional visits. Crab, Jerry, Thomas and Duke they would visits Mondays and Tuesdays. Harriett, Jack and Britain Wednesdays and Thursdays. Manrow, Shocky, Steve and myself-Page would visits the rest of the week.

84.   There was no way out for him getting any woman in the camp without being caught. The only escape would be when he got into town during his weekly trip taken by Mr or Mrs Faunally at their suppliers. Those hours that were missed out were not of any great consequences, since he was whether cooking or preparing the meal. For a week or two this was an ongoing watch and recrimination being over no substantial evidence that coming forward. Harriett told us that he had asked the cook about his family and the look he had given him was saying, 'I do not discuss my affair with other farm workers'.

85.   Thompson too has the same result that by looks he would or about the same age group like the cook, but they had no further in common apart from that age group. Things were getting to their boiling point on occasion even to be regular, not so much with the older married men but with the young studs of says about fifty percent out of the twenty overhauls. On Sundays staying in the camp would be like the hospital wards apart from playing the dominos, cards, bingos and little walk around the perimeter of the farm.

86.   The spread was limited for walks since we had covered the same walks over and over, being to the same place. Leaning on the same stump and almost throwing the same gravel as we timely walked along on Sunday afternoon and after dinner. One Sunday afternoon we had just started and Wiley and few of the others had left and gone out before us who were willing to walk while some were sleeping and leaving the walks for later. Standing at the door half open I saw two men coming in haste almost out of breathe saying, "those boys got into town last night. I just saw them going back and their boss is driving them. Believe me, Page it's true. It's them. It's true. What's wrong with us?" It was Harriett explaining jovially about the other group without hesitation.

87.   "That is shocking. Imagine they came after us and gone into town. Did they find any girls?" I enquired. "Yea, they must have got their weak light up. That's what it's about. That's what it's about. Vincent seems to

be happy, all of them." "Matthew, was he there?" "They didn't stop, but he wave and gone, and say he'll see us soon." By then Lewis passed and went into the camp to tell of their experience and about the other group being facilitated and had gone before us into town. For the cook apart he was still holding back and it probably was going to be more trouble of criticism for him than he had taught.

88.   "Shore, shore." Was the heave in the camp? "We're being treated like animals and not like hot blooded humans. What you say to that, cook?" From Harriett who was embolden to inquire and could vote. "You're all grown men, except for those two juveniles. You can whether go to town by yourselves or wait for the crop to complete." The cook stood up and pushed down his head and with both hands in his pocket. "It's only about six-seven weeks remain before the crops finish. I wouldn't take you nor does the liaison officer recommend it from past experience until the crop complete. The Lewis asks for that restriction because of past performance."

89.   "I bet if Matthew was in our group he would get through." I told him. "Because he's a communist agitator?" "No, because he understand me as a youth." Britain and I decided not to have supper for that evening because we were too upset, although it was available. The argument carries on, and on and looked forward for the crops to reap in, but the weeks seems to be stretching longer and longer and would not come nor end. This would be going over three months before

we would have seen any girls or women in the flesh although there would be in the movie on television. There were the Bonanza, Tombstone, Rawhide, Elliot Ness, Gun smoke, and Sugar Foot unlike the others. We fed well on these television programmes because there was nothing else to do on our time off.

- CHAPTER -
NINE

90.   We talked about them and fancy them, even to fall for girls that may have grown up and could be a great grandmother and probably were dead from old age, but that was all. The movie makers make it easy to show off their women and their girls but to us, who were watching it would be more serious and a fete. Before the travel I had a committed girl; we would ramp two or three times a day when it was convenient. Britain admitted that was the same with him and I got a letter from her the following Tuesday to say that she misses me terrible. She could not sleep without thinking about us together, after I read the letter I stuck it onto my body, just below my heart, but by the dinner time it was soaked with sweat and the ink blob it throughout.

91.   I tried to save some of it by laying it out in the sun to dry, but was to no avail. The other group owner lifted their restriction on going into town, one of the things he had done so was because his apple was late and not ready to be picked. Many of the time the men would be in camp all day or he would found them something else to do. Lifting the restriction was in his favour, probably avoiding any frustration, and beside they did not offer any incentives as to getting bonuses when the crop ends like we were. We learn this from the cook who seems to be getting a little bit friendlier than he was at first although the suspiciousness remains.

92.   Reflecting back when Barton question from the outset to the liaison officer was a good pointer. He and Manrow travelled previously and a few of them, like

others were married men, some were not but they have commitments to their girlfriends who may have a child or children back home. Others probably just seek quick dollars from the travel and keep themselves away from the conflict of the juveniles and the Afflicted. Crab and Bruce were from one of the other island and very seldom attune with us from the larger island and much more of us. Bruce drawn illicit arguments about his mirror that was laid on the bed when Britain sat on it and it shatters. He demanded a dollar for the mirror but Britain offered less and Bruce calls in the liaison officer to resolve the matter and when he came he awarded him two dollars instead. After that it was rumoured that the mirror was already broken and the amount awarded could have purchase four like mirrors. From then on there was a drawn sword against Bruce when he refused to return the two dollars to Britain claiming that his property was damaged.

93.   Little by little the older men were talking to us, and it was fun although they did not like losing the domino game, since Britain and I team up to play the older men. This they did not like at all and call us all the funny names they could think of when we won. Although they did not go to town and that idea seem to be whining I would still suspicious of them. They had nothing to lose except there return home and even Britain I place within that category. We did not get to spend any dollars during this time though there was lots of it around, being paid fortnightly with the first set of the bonus as promised.

94.   We commence to count down the days, but the days were too long at that point it was sixty three days to go that would carry us into the second week of October. October was a long way off to the end and anything could have happen during that spell. Some morning was very cold to our standard of having sunshine bountifully all of the time and round the clock. This was not disgraceful for even young men to feel the cold, and sometimes bring out their cigarette lighter to get a little warm from it in the apple orchard.

95.   I had a few more dollars, so how would I spend it going in town at the ending of the crop? What sort of women that I overheard the old men speak about I would get for my money. Would it be an old lady or a mother being middle age? Would she have her own chopper and looks like my girl that I left back home? I vowed that if I had another girl she would be her kind or better, but not below. No sir! Gleaning from older men this could happen having an older woman that back home would be looked up to and one, one did not fancy. They told us weird and wonderful stories of their escapade.

96.   Eight nine weeks or so ago I was going to glass, cleaning out gearboxes of whether the old Ferguson or from two, two twenty tonner Fargo and mud up to my eye in grease and sooth and smell of tainting like burning oil sump fluid. I could still smell the garage, the old oil and the overhaul sticky when I would squeeze myself in it. Mr C Jiles would be lecturing Tuesday and Fridays from morning until lunch then after I would go to meet

my girl. She would be there waiting with a little paper bag she shopped at Woolworth and a patty saved for me. She would still lick her lollypop or sucked paradise plumb and smile like she was like a queen, my queen.

97.   Someday I would be late back to the school, we had slipped into the Majestic where lovers make love at the movies and the time passed getting back. I would make up for it by working over late, but it was worth it. I held a red skin apple in my hand and play with it, and feel the smoothness of the skin it was lunch time and the supervisor called it out; we loaded onto the trailer that would take us back to camp for lunch. The cook asked me, 'Are you feeling well, Page?" I told. "I'm home sick, sick to my head."

98.   "You babies should not leave your mother." Steve quipped. "Man's job. What you looking for sympathy?" But before I could reply the cook jumped in and quiet down the seeming steamy development. However we went and collected our midday lunch. Everybody seems to be on high edge alert which descends into the crackling of plates, forks and knives aside from the gulping down the stew at the now middling of September. For some reason even the cook seem to be behaving unusual being on alert, and departed from the usual greetings he gives.

99.   Following the meal Thompson, Harriett and Duke leave the table early and although it was chilly they went outside through the double door seemingly discontent

about something hidden from Britain and myself. It was like the older bulls have their discussion without us the juveniles input and because the supervisor had taken Britain and I to a new field with luscious red apples they may have not taken akin to that being so. Whatever the reason that triggers the seeming discontent with that rank the air could be cut.

100.   Even when we loaded up the trailer and went back to the field there remain a flush of discontent weathering to explode in some sort of a hidden hanger. This mood lasted well through the evening and through the wash and right up until bed time and following the television shows which has been keeping us sane and humans. We had gone into our third months and we were told after that we can join the ranks from afflicted to being a fully farm worker. It was not a payment club but the accolade was automatically bestowing upon the new comer that has passes the test.

101.   We believe that it was design and formulated by older recruitees and have nothing to do with being legit. The rules may be reflecting way back to the nineteen forty four recruitments contract drive when young men felt more rebellious and suffers from that shock of leaving home. Young juveniles who had lost their young mother and father like me who lost my father at an early age too had no guidance from a father figure and some may not have mixed outside the immediate family until now and earning dollars, but could not be controlled after that.

- CHAPTER -
TEN

102.   Anyway, the men become subdued for the next day and Wiley who seem to be the more placid, Britain approach and inquire about the matter and what was bothering them. By now they had moved over to the new orchard with us: "Don't you hear what is happening? Boy, after you finish here we all are going to Vietnam to fight. To fight boy all of us, to fight." I overheard the conversation and jump in. "Our government agree to that?" "It could be a rumour, but is the supervisor tells us yesterday while you two was round here." Wiley continued and joined by Harriett. The others were swearing and saying that, "we are farm worker not an army." Manrow, who had some knowledge of the army life from serving a spell with British arm force shouted from the adjoining row, "They'll train you."

103.   The landscape was changing fast. Rumours go and come but they always give a possible intent and of something in the air brewing. Vietnam was not on our diet and although the liaison officer did not let us know the barrier has been drawn that he was compromising us to the yanks. That day right throughout the night and to the following day the conflict of that talk continues but without any official announcement has been made. The cook keeps to his saying that it was only rumours, and before anything like that happen Uncle Sam would have to sort it out with the British and that could take some time.

104.   He pointed out to me and Britain that we were the most likely they would chose, but that was another

spanner thrown in my life. Then it comes back to me that if I had stopped at mechanical school I would not have to consider joining the arm forces of another country outside our own. But Manrow was all for it and his enthusiasm regarding joining the yanks arm force to sort out North Vietnam could not come soon enough for him. I never missed watching clips from the aftermath of Second World War campaign, both in Europe and Japan on the television often on Sunday evening.

105.   The commentary was awesome and impressive with graphics includes ships aircrafts and men landing on land even the hand to hand combat. If so, meaning joining the US army forces, Britain and I had long discussion and women were no longer our priority anymore. Manrow had told us that we would be paid often time having nothing much to do since we would be like advisors and if at all we could join the engineering core and get indenture at the same time and getting paid for it.

106.   The reason being I need to be indenture before I was twenty one years old, else or somewhere around there, I may be too old and anything could happen to me after I get that piece of paper. This was a way out to satisfy my part of the family egos if the US wanted me into their army and I could join the engineering core. This was especially so if they get the ok from the British Empire office as my joining no longer depend upon my decision and could not have been since we were subject of the British sovereign, and beside I was still being a juvenile.

107.   Steve, Shocky, Bruce and Grab were slipping out after dusk on Fridays and Saturdays and not returning until late. They would slip out smartly and one evening we followed them and saw they were getting into a car that speeded off with them. When Bruce, joins the dispatching centre at Foxlake from Arkansas he brought some weight lifting equipment and pressing upwards of two third of his body mass. There would be some rumours flying about, since he was no longer interested in the weight lifting any longer, and that he was seeing a girl in town. Britain and I arranged to isolate Steve for information gathering for certain purpose but he would not budge anything.

108.   We had now clear eleven weeks out of the thirteen weeks that we were going to spend in Ohio State and no longer the time uncertain. I had spend sixteen weeks in total away from home by now and I learn to smoke, swears just for fun of it when I feel like it and question adults as though I been talking to some of my colleagues. I now the owner of prise black suit that I have no occasion for wearing yet and well over a thousand dollars in my case and in my pocket. Besides the security amount that was taken out as compulsory savings that were send home for us.

109.   The first impact of the others jeopardize my future behaviour were now pronounce in my hand that I could mingled with the bunch or group without fear of anything slipping out of hand. The danger was still there as the agreement with the Faunally's had not

been resend and could activated for some reason or the other as far as I was concern. Since we were not clear why this rumours persisted and for what reason they could be beside the bonus that was promised could enforce their agreement. This would be malicious since we almost reap in all of the crops and were now just gleaning orchard for late ripens.

110.   Reminding on what Mathew said about paying off Uncle Sam quickly would now for me just a one way stride. The apples fruit trees produce plentifully and bear luscious large fruits so that boxes would take less to fill. Payments earned per box and boxes were plentiful. We had now understood why restriction about the reaping in of the fruits crops was important, for any delay or time out would negate the crops from being fully and completed within the time given. So had we being allowed to go to town and any problems they had with us from drinks or other behaviour and were to return us home it would probably too late for recruitment to come through in time.

- CHAPTER -
ELEVEN

111.   The rumours as news were floating about in the camp that those who scanned the town saw girls and women, liquor joints, huge stores and shops packed with supplies they even met up with some from the other groups shopping. Some of them get as far as Cleveland and other places. The big push for reaping the crops has reduced to a trickle and on the twelfth week end we were allowed legally to go to town. Though quite a few of about fifty percent did not relish the idea of going into town that week end including the cook. We had considered why they would not come into town with us, and ponder whether they were crooking up things for us as the thought run through our mind.

112.   There were three taxis pulled up outside the camp and some of those who were not going came out to wave as we were on our way to meet the town for the first time. I did not wear my suit although this was one of my first occasions visiting the city. I wore a wrangler and a black short sleeve shirt with a white stripe coming down from the collar in sleek silk finish. The purchase of this perfect deco coming from Wisconsin and suited for the occasion. The other two taxis had gone on before us as we followed behind only occasionally glimpsing the rear tail lights of the one in front.

113.   Then after sometime we arrived in town, we called it town since if we had gone to the city; to Cleveland it would have taken several hours and sometime to reach there. The older men of the group agreed that we should all stay in the nearby town for the first time. The

reputation of our group still could hang in the balance since there were uncertainty what liquor and women could provoke and the response. A few questions were thrown at the juveniles, Britain and I about our drinking habits and how we feel under the liquored, but I told them that I was and hard rum drinker, Whisky, Gin, Brandy milk stout and Guinness since I was a baby. I know them all and nothing in Uncle Sam's country could outflank the sting brew of white rum.

114.   My older sister told me that at night when I rise up everybody for food in the home that was what they gave me to drink white rum turn down a little. Sometime it would be midday before they hear a sound out of me when I was really annoying. This was relay to the men who question me so that they could take a measurement from my experience of rum and the baby drinker, and that I could hold my liquor. The bonus payment would not include the earned wage and would only pay when the building checks on we were on the coach that would take us to the main greyhound station. Britain was not that sort of child he explains that he drinks for social reason and that he did not like drinking.

115.   I was acclaimed to be the youngest and still a juvenile and inexperience youth, but had grown quickly and after the taxi unloaded I was called by, 'pits, pits' to speak to one from the other group. It seems that he was talking to Matthew who may have asked him to look out for the juveniles. He was our guardian who took me and Britain behind a liquor store and opens a door and asked

us to climb the stairs that leads to some rooms. Now we had to use our imagination to read about language accurately. It was like, "twenty five dollars a session get in cut the ribbon, ten minutes out." A woman was there, seems not to be much older than my girl home, but there was no time to ponder cause of the time scale.

116.   When I leave it was Britain waiting anxiously at the door with the same wording as they used for me. I had ponder why they let the juveniles goes in firstly, since we were at that stage to bring hurt to those sessions because of our youthfulness and egos? But that was how it was allotted. She had a hard time with Britain since he wanted to have two sessions at the same time but she would not allow it, and almost causes a riot at the door which the older men back at camp were concern with. After the visits and we had a few drinks and went to do night shopping. We did not hit our pillows until daylight for the Sunday morning when we would listen to all the gags and tales from the evening out.

117.   The thirteen weeks came to its end followed by several visits to Youngstown. My black suit now have a case to rested in instead of everybody seen it hanging on the wall over the bed. Mr and Mrs Faunally and their daughter came up to the camp and paid us our earned wages and bids us goodbyes. When the coach was loaded he came onto the coach and handed to all of us envelope that contained the bonus payment he had promised. We counted as they were good people, but they had got bitten and they were not going to let

it happen to them again, 'so it was once bitten and twice shy.'

118.   We had now reached the greyhound station where we aboard for the Southern United States, Florida at Leesburg dispatching centre. This was travelling for days on this huge coach, travelling night and day, sleeps and woke up and Matthew was back. On the coach some were saying about their escapade, but we had find out that those from the other orchard had not been so well paid because the crops was not well bear enough as where we were. A few of them did not even commence to repay for their airfare of the eighty four dollars it cost and also their living expenses much more to have so many dollars in their pocket going down south as most of us were from the Faunally contract.

119.   Mathew was not forthcoming as when we first met at the Foxlake complex, although he did not showed any coolness towards me he was nevertheless low steely. The bunch that he was with may have sapped his forth comeliness and over the thirteen weeks I was not with him, he gradually developed a degradable and lonely streak. Where I notice he was less talkative on an opening subject I reduces it but provided him with another solution to talk, but he was not going to have it and remains aloof to my effort the two to three days and nights on the greyhound.

120.   He could have been annoyed by poking fun about him being a communist by his colleagues, in democratic

states earning the dollars with, 'in God we trust,' written on every coin. Then the player on the world scene might have been 'Premier Nikita Khrushchev, President Eisenhower, Prime minister Harold McMillan and General De Gaulle, with President Nasser came on the scene with other pawn trying to grab other headlines or two. In my little time in the world and very much shallow and inexperience it did not allow me to stretch my imagination to that far about politics and what they do to influence turn of events. If join the US army as advisors to the south Vietnamese I would needed a year or two before they could send me off to Vietnam. I had not the slightest idea about wars then, though I guess I could learn the ropes.

121.   Though Matthew seems to be quiet I believe he still would entertain and visit my young lives again, but needs time. Boys beyond my age back home would called themselves or refer to others as being a comrade but the seeming animosity being shown to Matthew by the adults appears that adults uses it to make an impact on those who consider comradeship to be wholesome. The less than a year, I could reflect on Mr Jiles comment that travelling will widen my horizon and make me to be a better person although he was talking to all of us in general. Now I had to cope with the indifferences and filtered and re-filtered out the bad part of this growing up experience.

122.   As time spent on the greyhound more or less was unobtrusive it had given me time to reason about the

things I have gone into. I learn to smoke, swear, paid for sexual intercourse with probable older women that I did not indented and having dollars in my pocket that I earned with my two hands. I send money home for my mother and some of the family that I had. If I did not take this tripped I would not otherwise have it to give them. Although probably later on when I passes out and have my indenture and took work that was payable.

123.   Now about joining the American army as advisors in Vietnam it seem that, that idea or rumours were unfounded and nothing was said about this feature has been said again. So getting into the engineering core was a myth dreamed up and polished rumours although I did not wanted to hear, but understandably so to benefit me and my future prospect. Manrow did not mention nor show any of his previous enthusiasm he had and judging from the lack of information automatically killed the seeming rumours off. I also notice that my thinking mostly dwells externally about things that a few months ago did not consider as important. We had now passing through the State of Georgia a southern state that was believed to be segregationist state. The greyhound stopped at a motel and the driver asked us to give a list of what we wanted as refreshments and warned us not to come off the coach and particularly to be quiet.

– CHAPTER –
TWELVE

124.   It was about midnight when we were on the motel site. Someone like a security guard inquire about the passengers from the driver, "these are British Boys going to Florida." He told him. Because of my respect for Matthew anything he was saying I would listen keenly so much so that when he completed what he has to say I could repeat almost word for word. This might have been how influential men gain their upper hand over the young like I was and he was saying. "Watch out, you're in lynching country now." He did not expand anymore than so and remain quieter than his usual self.

125.   By then the driver ordered and was waiting. For precaution he locked the door while he was waiting, he did not do so when we stopped at the motel in the north. But now it was all precaution and when they bought the bags with the refreshments he handed it and immediately driven away. The lights remain dimed to almost turning off on the coach besides the highway lights. Wiley and few others were commenting about the treatment of the American citizen, their own. This I could not naively understand but for a while it becomes clearer about the predicament we could have involved in.

126.   It has frightened me considerable as we drove along and the highway due south. This was not part of the experience that Mr Jiles wanted me to experience, and if he did then he might have warned about those frightening situation that existed out there also. I left space for Matthew to re-entered with my continue learning, but he was cautious. Manrow held a few tips

too on mostly about his army experience, and could not stray any distant from that experience. Britain on the other hand behave almost like he was only interested in boys talk and did not stray nor bother one way or the other to stretch his imagination further.

127.   Shortly the greyhound reported problems and the driver report a detour before we could clear Georgia State. It remains hairy at least while we were at the garage. However we had unloaded to the change of another vehicle but it was warmer then than uppermost north we were coming from and by now it was early morning daylight. The garage staffs were on hand or so it seems to guide us to the vehicle that would take us to Florida State, at Leesburg the distributing centre. A few of our colleagues were sneezing, which could be owning from coming off a warm coach into a different temperature, but it was not how some of the previous and long term visitors on contract view their sneezing buddies. They were whispering about their women back home which I did not clearly understand.

128.   When the vehicle was loaded I ask if I could swap for little while on the seat beside Matthew. I had two things to discuss with him, the first that he being a communist and what it meant. The second besides other smaller matters but who they refer to being 'Joe Grind?' Both question could brings controversy if expanded on, but Matthew was the first one like he was waiting for me with matters too to discuss. "You told me that you are a communist-what that is?" I asked just as the coach

return back onto the main highway due south. If there was a learned chamber to catch anything going then I must be was carrying it onto my head like buck growing its first horn and to collect and gathered them all.

129. "You heard of Karl Marx?" "Yes, I heard of him, but I don't know anything about him. He lives in Russia somewhere." "Karl died sometime, years ago now, he was a good philosopher and lead a band called communist or communism." "They're Russian aren't they?" "Yes, but the yanks hate them because they called them the iron curtain people." "What they do their, make iron?" He looked at me as though I was stupid. "That's not what it means. It means that they avoid anything coming from the West. They view the west with suspicion meaning the yanks that's part of the western countries."

130. "Who is the mysterious man they keep on calling him named 'Joe Grind?" "Who tell you about him?" "Most of the other men use it especially when one of them sneeze, the others would laugh and told him that-is he a bad man?" "You've got a girl?" "Yea-beautiful thing she is, Barbara her name is, a school teacher's daughter." "Who did have her before you?" "No body, actually I don't know about that." The man was listening in the seats before ours he was from Matthews' camp. "Makes big men cries. Joe Grind he is a killer, a cuckold of a man but he's a sweet boy. Never done a day's work in his life but always have money to burn. He done things on timing, precise timing."

131.   "Who's your friend Matthew?" by then he had entered into the conversation whether he was invited or not he was there in it. Notches himself on the seats in the same row. "Tell the youth, the true story." He told Matthew. "If he's not going to I'll tell you." This greyhound was a different type from that we originally set off from Ohio State with being upstairs, now this one was one level. Everybody could now join in and throw their penny worth in the conversation with own stories to tell about the man called 'Joe Grind. They took over that story so much so that there was no part for me to in-depth study being it, him or her nor learn about it, him or herself. I guess because the elders refer to being him, I concluded that it must be him a male gender of a sort. But I would listen keenly to feed my hungry learning skills.

132.   The story raised continued to be very hot, since the men was discussing his escapade for hours as the coach travels and sways thorough the hills and valleys to our over a thousand miles destination and journey including the detour. Being on my own stage I then commented loudly about the State we were still in and what segregation meant, but the time and the elders were more concern and consumed about 'Joe Grind' than anything else. It was passionate discussion so much so that laughter ensued. I was feeling elated since I raised the issue, and although I could not grasps some of the contents this discussion gave me a wider view of inspecting 'Joe Grind' from a perceptive angle.

133.   What I gathered is that 'Joe Grind' had a status of being an entity. A man of many discrete talents but he was mostly interested in women who their husbands or boy friend were absent away for a short while or longer from home. He would press the women into having favours so that he could consume them with gifts of kindness and whirl himself into their hearts and lives. It did not matter from which continents, island, race, social status or background this concept happens to be, there, and always be a 'Joe Grind' trying to get his way and commit an act. His way was to take unintentional care of the women in laudable way and for him to spend some or all the fund sent back home. The marker for the men then would become obvious by his sneezing, and how he does it and his precept of his family determination as has being the case would determine by, JG.

134.   When the original coach took the detour the cook that was with us went over to a car that had just pulled up outside the station, being gesturing but could not be heard of what he was saying. A case came up back at the camp. The cook did not show any feelings regarding the male and female composition. Some were suggesting that because he knows the rule that he was working against and had help to sidetrack against us having women in the camp. Meanwhile the car was driven off before we commence to load the greyhound and we have never seen it again.

135. However, the cook was saying, "This wife, I leave her to go nowhere, 'cept when I'm working, she travels with me all the time north to south. I leave her nowhere on her own." It was Wiley's voiced uplifted the laughter, "You mean you've been having it off all the while you were starving, denying us?" The cook continued, "She was in Cleveland all the time, I go to see her every week. Sometimes twice." "O, yes. You're a very secretive man. Can't be trusted, can you?" Wiley told him and laughed heartily. "I have to be, I knew that all of you was watching me at camp. You're not the first to do so. I can play a game or two too." Wiley, who were the more lively on the subject retorted quickly with some comments by inform murmur, "Don't tell me that you're afraid of Joe Grind too?" It was the cook that partially had the last say with Matthew consented, "I told you about them. That's what happens to me. That's why my boy didn't have my name because of Joe Grind. He took my home over, my dog and my wife she just got up and leave, just as I leave. Very enterprising. "

136. Matthew did not like the recourse of telling his side of the story, but since he belongs to the communist party, he could not or supposed not to hold back his thoughts. But then he was in predicament in that sense neither could he be frank too much about an whole, since he himself may not of understood the full diametric of communism. Another thing too he knows that he was laying out milkiest from the others that he would be with for the rest or of this part of his living life on

the contract. The first thing that some cruel person will refer to and presumable might argue he could not satisfied his wife's needs and that was why Joe Grind got the upper hand. I guess that was why he behaves more subdued when we met again and not being his usual self.

137.   In respect for Matthew I did not enjoy laughing at those carnal swipes the others now poked and enjoy from the predicament of a man who had good intention. I consider he would be at sometime hits out at those who were mimicking, but he did not. For a short while, I commence to reason about where I was going. Although I am now well into few months of becoming into sort of manhood the realisation of returning home without my own roof over my head, no trade indenture and probably without the girl I had left behind now belonging to Joe Grind, though I could not be certain. This was dauntingly frustrated.

138.   Within a few months it seems as though Matthew's predicament about my staying on longer in Uncle Sam's country reduced the possibility. The contract debt was almost paid off leaving only a few dollars to complete. Owning from the rich apple crops of the chard in Ohio and the determination of the owner to gathering in all of the crops. Had the owner leaves us to go on to the city regularly it was possible that we would not have earned so much dollars, but his crops would not completely reaped. Along those lines of reasoning, I conclude that after they were satisfy with

our performance, he paid us and that was that. They had no further responsibility regarding us after they had turn us over to the next contractor.

139.   It was uncertain after coming to Florida where we would end up. At sugar plantation I was told that it was unyieldingly hard. The orange and grapefruit, if there was good farmer, then dollars could be earned. If the farmer was not so good and not taking care of his fruit trees then there was hardly any crops with the level of satisfying earning could be had. The southern States earned less than the northern states per capita we were told. Sometimes it the crop does not bear well, the contracted will spend much time in the camp eating and drinking and living off credits. The bad earnings of some and by their accumulative credits make sure review with certainty those would be returning to north again to help pay off their debts.

- CHAPTER -
THIRTEEN

140. Mulling over Matthews counselling now shows some resemble alignment of his sturdiness and truthfulness too. With only a few dollars to be paid off, even so I might as well did not work so hard to accumulate these amount since it could have been spent off and still reminded of what Mr Jiles saying passively. "I've seen men returns without anything in their suitcases or trunks." Mathew said. "You're working too hard, reduce it." And the farmer said. "We won't let you go until you've reaped every one off the trees. If you do we'll pay you good and more."

141. Within few minutes we were unloading at the Leesburg despatching centre. The arguments and counter arguments about JG could go on and on, but could not do so because the priorities had now changed. Men were sorting out their trunks and suitcases and looking for places to rest and bunked down for the night. The operation was carried out as army like. With names and numbers bellows through mouth pieces assist loudhailers. More greyhound were coming and going as fast as they unload their occupants. Seems through Britain and I travels together we were called together and might have because we were the younger in our team and gets on well.

142. We were to Get to our quarters quickly, and have a shower and get down to the mess hall as soon and as quickly as possible also. Everything becomes a must do for the team we were joined to. Any deviation meant there could be no breakfast, lunch nor dinner served and

no excuse for missing the time given. Time missing were not allowed, neither throwing away meals no matter how terrible it tasted, look or served. Everybody accounts just for himself only. Even the water to have a shower smells different it was very sulphated and many of those of us who travel directly to the north some were having problems with the smell, even though I did not of myself.

143.   Shortly we were in the mess hall, men were sitting down chatting and laughing away as I grabbed a tray and find my way up to the servers. Britain came in too followed by the other rest of twenty of us excluding the cook and they did the same. As I moved along the queue I notice that those that followed behind form treble bends of S's. Those Servers seems to be working flat out as more and more men joins the queues. After another short while I went on to sits down at a wide straight table with the seats a long bench and the table join together. Not all twenty of us could be seated at this table but looking around I notice that they all were sitting down and meeting their colleagues who may have came in from those different states and telling their stories too. Some were old travellers. They would scan their story and mention some of the terrain and experience they had.

144.   The tale of JG was quite common coming from old and new travellers alike and even the concept of those who were being harmed remain the same. They would describe his escapade but have varying ending and circumstantial antidote would put into the mixture

to give the story a plausible course. We did not have time to share mush about JG and the burning issues that have befall travellers because straight away we were summons to get our things together within few minutes to spare. Now the songs have been change too, the song of "A man Shook up" imbedded into the hit parade to replace with 'O Carole I but fool and the ongoing rock & roll.'

145.   The travel this time was far different from what we had up north. It was a truck with hard seats benches slings into unbolted rows with a canopy covered shelter and a back board letting in just enough daylights. When the vehicle stops or slows or bumps, round corners those seats move along not in straight line but according to movements of the vehicle with the passengers applying pressure in any direction to compensate. It was far from being comfortable and the driver seems disinterested about the cargoes he was carrying.

146.   The movement was quickly and compactly executed so it was uncertain who was on the vehicle in the eighteen who were in this group and if they were any of the originals included my-self, I did not know who were positively there. After an hour or so we had reach the camp where we were going to spend some time with this farmer. We were glad to unloaded and refresh our bones by stretching and twisting to put them back into their rightful places. Any flesh that had grown on our bottoms was of little comfort because of rapid movements on the wooden seats. It was bum, bum, bum, nostalgia.

147.   It was dusty campus yard with a large building stood out on with white maul surrounding it. We had now climb three steps carrying our luggage through a secondary door to enter the building itself. They put on a welcoming party from those who were permanently staying at the camp and quickly show us around and help us to get familiarise with the place. It was believed to be summer, but then it was quite cloudy from missile from the Cape Canaveral centre had just gone off not too far away from the camp site. All this from conviction of learning new things.

148.   They had taken only two of us from the original twenty at the Ohio contract and one from the nearby farm. Matthew was not with us anymore neither CC nor Harriett, but only Britain of the others. It looked out of place since now we all would be cooking for ourselves. No new laundries, no meal in the evening preparation for us, and the shopping too all had to be done. Many, information come fast somewhere good and others could be leave for some other time. I learn never to reject any free given information outright since it may becomes useful for another time. Mr Jiles told us that we should not reject anything quickly but mull it over, because we may need the same information to help ourselves latter.

149.   The smell and taste of diesels and its fumes had almost gone. My nails would somehow keep clean and I could see the ten quits deep down around the finger nails. My boots no longer filled or soaked with oil and

grease on under their bottom looking back on whose floor had to be clean up after I had walked over it. These and others were replacements of a kind. A sort of swapping one for another and weighing up the pros and cons. Some were neither here nor there. But, others make great differences because I had not gain a lot of income at that moment to replace what I exchange my indenture for.

- CHAPTER -
FOURTEEN

150.   We were on the camp site now gone two weeks without drawing a straw. The farmer crop was not yet ready and we had to eat and drink accordingly. This would be from our savings that accumulated from the north that we were digging into, and besides the credit arrangement for the living accommodation as well. At the Cape missile were going off regularly to rock us almost out of our bed at night and during the day we would watch them going up followed by the trail of smoke tail through the atmosphere. It has gone sometime now since I hear from home. I have some based dates that we were going to leave the north. I had time to write letters home but even if any reply letters were on their way before I told them back home, it would still gone north before it could be trace back to Leesburg and find us eventually.

151.   Gathering the information from those who stayed at the camp continuously about the farmer and his crops that we were with was not very encouraging. His crop was less produce than the brother. Besides the fruit trees were much taller and even taller ones that were called the 'valenchas'. The common tall fruits trees normally used the seventeen ft ladder, but on the valenchas the requirement was over and above forty eight ft. This means that we had was to work double harder now than ever before to earn little to keep and to purchase food. The bags carrying the fruit were larger and the boxes to measure the fruits were also larger than the apples and as much.

152. Often I heard men shouting about their bags that they were feeling like donkeys. Howbeit it was like an escape route. I had now learned almost all the words of profanity and could use them to mixes up and even to reflect my feelings like treads running through my new vocabulary. I now sure that if my mother and others hear me then they would not entertain me in their homes anymore. I was not afflicted anymore and those newly ones that came in overnight directly from the islands would treat the same as I was treated when I was afflicting myself too.

153. "To escape the afflicted name calling," Matthew said. "You have to travel north even once. And then when you go to the south, you're no longer afflicted, but a fully fledge UNCLESAM's potentiate. It could be visa-versa. The experience of the two sides you must have. See the people and see the country. Big country." He commented. All along he cared and watched over my travel for the little time I known him and being together. Now for some months we hardly talked or heard him gripe according to his feelings which mostly were sensational and often refer to outburst of some sort of another with laughter ensued haughtily from the other colleagues. Though they avoided him most times he had genuine ego which clarifies his heart condition and whether he was being liked or not there was a value he had which I like about him.

154. Recalling some of the passing inference of Mr Jiles that it was like in the army. "Today you meet

someone whom you like and knitted together straight away. You built up that repos and soon you or him parted never to see each other again. It's like that. Sometime you've written to inquire about him to your former head quarters. If you do get back a reply it could be devastating. At first I would do it, but soon I began to get use to the idea and live with it. I commenced soon," he would sigh heavily and paused, "but you treated all colleagues as temporary friends."

155.   I realised the implication of the dilemma that ensued from the pointer view of Mr Jiles. And my particular was not deep in view of experience with regards to missing Matthew and the paused and sigh that tells about something hurtful about the experience of Mr Jiles. He did not reminisce in recalling his time in the arm forces at what age he was called up to service. But, now that I was still between nineteen and twenty years of age I could clearly observe as part way up the seventy eight ft ladder to get the fruits, about my future destiny.

156.   It was the roaring from the Cape and missiles that has gone up that make me becomes weary of the height I had been up climbing and dismounting with bags full of fruits. Other men were doing the same on the other rows adjoining, and then moving the ladder by rolling it across from tree to three, dear not to let it falls. It had taken three men at times to get it up and almost an hour before every one could commence to get the fruits. This is what available and what I got. Then

it becomes an exchange with this going up and down ladders instead of sucking oil, diesel out of sump and rocking out joints out of the bearing housing followed by hammering to complete the operation.

157.   Planning was not an issue, since the farmer is the one that done this and get men to do his job and I was part of that man making up his team. It was a dollar and one cent per box paid for the fruit and just might pick four of five boxes per day, others may pick more or less. That just clears thirty dollars and few cents per week. Not much to pay for food and laundry and for savings. I still owed seventeen dollars and some cent. The last payment made on the fair was out of my last pay day from Ohio the northern states. Not much was going on in the orange and grape fruit picking regarding good pay pocket.

158.   The cash was running out fairly and regularly dipping into the accumulated resource that had come from saving. The last time I check the bills in my case there was not much left in the pile that now worn down into closing hallow when I squeezed my fist. Not bigger than the roll of a good spiff. Those who had started the crops at the Green Giant plant at the start of the crops could stand the reduction in earnings and thaw it out. But those like me who had gone in at the tail end of the crop see our resource reducing considerable, with only a few hundred dollars left. We were eating it out in the southern state.

159. "I saw men coming back from the United States with only their suitcase and pair of wrangler on their back and few pounds of their compulsory saving at McDonald." Mr Jiles alluded to the greatest hit and misses of travelling. I wish now that I had not listened to Mr Jiles inferences and experiences. But since I could not purchase it, I would learn from my mistakes and doings. Still having over a year or so before becoming an adult. Although it was a good time to make mistake and re adjust it also could leave a juvenile with colour of intent. By making bad mistakes that could not be readjusted. Far, from days when mums clip's me around the ears on occasionally when I slipped out of place, she just realigned and reset my thinking.

— CHAPTER —
FIFTEEN

160.   After two weeks the valenchas fruits were completed and we moved into more prosperous field that we could now earn a little more weekly. It still did not put more on the spending plate but halt and stable the spiffs' roll, so that I could get pocket money out of it. The bothering thoughts of what 'have I done' would continue at the dawn of each day. My, first decision making machine was observable staggering for catastrophic collapsing and nothing I fiscally could do about it besides going along with being hopeful.

161.   By this time I heard that Matthew with some of the originals from Ohio State was near Orlando picking fruits, but how he himself was prospering was not given and based upon hear-say. Although, he was skill in his reasoning and seems know when to poise and when not to I was still missing him even though we were together for a short while. If anything I believe happens to me he would be coming from anywhere he was, but then it could be my inexperience that leads me to conclude that this would be so. That was my first knitting outside my family circle and seems would be short lived, since he never try to keep in touch. I concluded that from Matthews experience if he had wants to he would already the first to tell me where he was and getting on.

162.   It was not a bother for Matthew since his aim was to spend the full three years limit in Uncle Sam's country by not working hard to pay his keeps. I was gradually being aware of his council, but being young and very agile I could not bear to hold off longer than

what was done and since. Wherein now that I had simplified youthful mistake, but still having regrets if so it may be possible I might return with a suitcase full with Uncle Sam's stale air and few dollars at the point of payments one month later. Albeit, the orange crop was too lost a little bit longer then than the contract at the Ohio apple.

163.   It was on a Friday afternoon when three men came to the camp some months later. I was having a shower when Britain calls and told me that I was wanted, and insisted that I should hurry up and come along. Then I got dress and went out into the kitchen where they were now holding a meeting. Not long my name was called and the security number accompanying the call out. Those who their names did not call must leave the meeting at once. Then one of the men was saying, "You are selected to join as advisor to the United States army in South East Asia, Vietnam, you'll be notified shortly when we'll call you. This is briefing." One of the citizens told us before they went.

164.   The two men did not take question nor ask for any. It was a matter that the decision was a cut and dried conclusion. All nine of us that were selected after the men drove away we too concluded that that was so. This has given a sort of elation for the reason that it would be possible to join the engineering and logistic advisory team. I already got some sort of hands on apprentice practices with practical knowledge of engines, particularly of large and heavy equipment and theory

that would have considered suitable for the position. I already done over two years in this environment and the business of identifying various make and model of engines and parts would be evident. I was living and sucking oil and liquid from engines, best part since leaving school.

165.   It seems that I would be achieving my goal at last, if I did not get wounded or killed in the mean time doing so. It was locked up leaving my family that I had made the right decision and probably coming back whether in bag or achieved something in the US army. Besides coming back with nothing in the suitcase and a wrangler trousers and skimpy jacket as a traveller would be a shamble. With whatsoever were being considered I would be willing to go along without any objection so long as it gives me a leeway in the meantime and simplified my future.

166.   But then, I may have travel too for in the distant from the time the message were delivered by those two men to rectify the recrimination that awaits if I failed one way or the other. I could visualise Mr Jiles to say, "I told you so. I knew that this would happen." He would gloat's. And how about others who heard that I was doing so well ahead of my colleagues? Now that I had failed in whatsoever I was doing well in with? What would Governor Henry Morgan think if he's been around at this point? Would Morgan enact objection regarding the crown subject joining a foreign arm forces to be advisor in another foreign land for it?

167.   Since we were closer to the United States than United Kingdom someone suggested that: "The Crown his getting bags of revenue from us being working in the United States. And joining the US army would bring even more revenue." One of the older men told us that was not one of the nine. If this had happen when we were in North America then Manrow an army man would tell us of the certainty when they would call us up for service and probably tells about the training that we would get or receive.

168.   Little by little I would tweak in my youthful dreams about the future and what I were going to be. Based on everything else goes according to plan and whether I survive and return home. I still having just over a year when I would be legally a man and not responsible to answer to anyone. I could choose to marry and vote or not to vote and get marry to Julie Rose or some other girl. But, according to what I heard about travelling it can be itchy and drew a stigma depending on what happen overseas with one or to one. Returning home with a bag full of goodies, and medals crown with gold could become a friend of the Priminister or to some higher elite in the country of origin.

169.   It was, how to survive and get back home with something to show from the absent from the country. Whether it is a large country or continents the stigma and contents remains regarding close friends and family. That was how I weighed it up, and I believed that it was not too far off from the actual fact. Matthew

who had schooled me for a short while on travelling was not available. Since we came down south it seems that something had gone missing. The friendship and friendliness that present itself at first had disappeared and neither the older ones in the camp seems bothered one way or the other. Only time that one may exchange and communicate was at the stove when making breakfast or cooking at evenings. In the kitchen the stove and wash hand basin were five rows of ten columns with men cooking and chatting away. The new ones like us the older men would shows us to light the stove and where we get the cooking utensil, such knives fork and spoon provided by the camps they would pointed out.

170.   Very little input as far as I was concern related to social interaction has been done to ease any discomfort or take place. We were not even refers to as being immigrants, which would have given a status, but as farm workers. The interests of the men were mostly to get to the orange or grapefruit grove the next day. They smoked and go to bed for an early morning rise. It was six groups of us in the camp working for six different fruit growers. A noticeable development pattern off the growers who's had better crops, those men docked themselves as the elite amongst the others. Hot as it were for women when we were up north, it was hardly mention now that few of us could save and have any dollars accumulated since our arrival.

- CHAPTER -
SIXTEEN

171.   The young juveniles were still restless, since it means going into Orlando and few of the older men says that getting women even for a session was costing them more than it was up north. I checked my peal with Britain and he had fewer dollars left on his piles than I had. I put away my roll and promised that I would not pull off anymore even if had to starve, beg or sell my suit to Britain who at this point could not afford it either. Although he often ask me to sell the suit to him when we were in Ohio it bother him less it seems and may have mention it only once or twice since we came to Mims some months gone. If he did have a hundred dollars to pay then for the suit he could have had it, but he did not clear eighty dollars on his pile.

172.   Britain may have just had enough in his pocket now to hire a taxi to take him home from the airport if the farmer should call it a day and send us directly home. Our fair and keeps, owed had now reduce to twelve dollars and some cents to completed. Our group with four others would be going, so the rumour has it and we did not know where or when this would take place. There would be three of those of us that were named from the nine to join the US army. That would leave them at the camp to finish gleaning the grove of its crops when the time comes for us to depart. The regularity of cards playing and dice rolling increased was evident as the gambling to reduce or gained from those who were staying and from those who were going. It went on late into the night.

173.   After many days passed six from those of the groups went that was chosen to join the US army. They were told about their going to other contractor places the next day. They woke up early and before we leave with our crew those that were leaving stood outside as wonderingly and anxiously waiting. Those ladders that they had usually carried to the grove packed up and lying a little away in heaps outside and along the camp undisturbed. Also those seventy-eight feet ladders too were lying there with some grasses commence to sprouted out and grown tall through the steps and soon needed to clean up before being overtaken. How much dollars they left or taken with them from those left over at the camp can only be surmise.

174.   The roaring activities that evening when we got back were missing and the camp seems only a third of the men were left. The stoves and the kitchen activities were reduced considerable. Inquiring from the camp supervisor and getting anything out of him was known to be hard work and where the men were sent becomes even harder. However, soon somebody would be told about those men true fate a week or two following there leaving out of the camp.

175.   I was not even a sympathiser of communism simply because I did not know what it was nor even the depth, nor shallow of the concept. Since I could not vote nor taken part in any saying of adults it did not bother me in one little bit. But, any who take interest in my affairs especially adults and treated me fairly that

person was considered by me as a friend. This might be taken as selfishness but that is how it would pan out for a long time even throughout adult life. It might be owing to how adults treated me or talk to me during my early years that I secretly developed a dislike and likeness depending on the view taken in favour or not for them.

176.   So in the sense that I would be called 'a Matthew's sympathizer' would be ludicrous in the sense that although Matthew would refer to me as a comrade which I did not even response in kind to calling him comrade in return. 'That was adults for you,' I reasoned, and reasonable told me so. Just over a year and something, I would become an adult whether I stayed on the contract or not this was unavoidable. The decision I made to go on contract would be counted that I avoid getting an indenture and also equate the running decision of the juvenile mind. This was most puzzling, because seldom would my adult elders reasonable talked to me without compromise my time with their instruction without a grunt and groan as to say, 'why bother telling him something like this, that he'll find out anyway.' 'Or you're coming, you'll see.'

177.   New to me was the ever learning that must be involved whether I like it or not. Most times it comes without trying as I commence to learn new things every daylight hours I awake. Matthew has influence my thoughts in a short time we were together, even to the depth that he himself might not evidence how far

reaching it was even as he used to say, 'if you live in a community then you're a communist, as simple as that.' Though others might take this simple analogy to a higher level of doubt other from Matthew views of the whole issues. It seems that it was not hard to find person who would take reckless issues for the like of doing so continuously, even as far as to pick a quarrel about Matthew's political views, although he had none. The views of adults were cumbersome for my juvenile growth. They put in my head that I might worry about growing up and the future even without trying.

178.   Pointing to clearer picture of what it would be like when I become a man, was another sidekick in the form of a man called Burtie Campbell. I wanted to sell insurance policies while at mechanical school to help out and provide more spending. A sale position was advertised in the local news paper for person to sell insurance policy for one of a well known insurance company in the corporate area. The advertisement carried a piece about the earning potential for one evening work. When I finish the evening, I met Julie Rose and we walked downtown to the office where the interview was being held.

179.   When it was my turn to see Mr Campbell he told me to take a seat and shook my hand. Then at first he seems to be a friendly man but his questioning would be about my future, "Mr Page, what you're doing now, at this moment?" "Doing motor mechanic at Jiles school sir." "You've completed the course?" "No, is my second

year." "You're going to completed it, aren't you?" "I would like to, yes." "Tell me why you want this job?" "I want to earn some money, so that I can buy my family present." "All of your family, and after that?" The adult laughed haughtily and looked at me thoroughly.

180. "What about your parents, do they think the same?" "I don't know about that. Never discuss with them." "Want to get a sneaky job behind their backs, are you?" "No." "What else, can think about you and your parents? Hard working people. Send you to school. Paying for you to attend mechanical school. Feed and cloths you, and now Mr Page you're trying to sneak one in on them. I tell you what I am going to do for you and your parents. I am not going to give you this job. You see when you grow up,' he said, 'a trade is the best thing to have."

- CHAPTER -
SEVENTEEN

181. "Mr Page, you'll able to look after your family when you're married and have a wife and children. You'll be ready to try other things if things going wrong, but at any time you can return to your trade. You're your own man. This is why I'm not going to give you this job. And my advice is to stick to your trade. Stick to your trade. Stick to your trade. Next?" He shouted, for the next interviewee then he rise and shook my hand again and bid me good buy and good luck to me and my trade. That was how I come to be not having a job.

182. Julie Rose waits for me during the interview, but she did not know one way or the other if I got the job. I did not tell her straight away or directly, as I had promised her that dress in the Wong Chung store down town on Princess Street. It was what they called then 'the ballerina dress.' She would be wearing it when we were going to meet. That was the idea. I probably should have hold off until I got the job. But I did promise and forced the promotion both in my mind and seeing her dressed up in it so much so that this job was a cert.

183. As I plucked the oranges from the limb I pondered what if I got back without being better off economically. The crops were replenishing rapidly and scantily. Few boxes of orange daily, and paid by a few dollars. We were gleaning the field for fruits to put in boxes that could not be filled. Early in the day we would return back to the camp having nothing to do but gaff, smoke and ponder and watching our buying power reduce and rumours rife among the campers. I cocked my ears to

hear anything that would calm my anxious deliberation. Some of it was about wild boars roaming the Florida everglades. And that we should go out hunting for the armadillos and wild boars or else we are going to starve.

184.   How truthful that concept were, would only proven by being friendly to one of the native American who held a hunting rifle and probably a licence to hunt those animals. Those that secure their stay summer and winter at the camp have friends of that nature and would seek their help. The hunts was being arrange during week end only. Those that were going on the hunt would be picked by the camp supervisor and charged with the safety for those who were on the hunt.

185.   The first week end produce only one armadillo, hardly enough to share and for any beside the one caught the animal. This did not need a rifle to kill the beast except to dig it out of its hole and carefully pulled it out. There was an exception to my stomach about eating the meat of the armadillo, and since I did not go on this hunt. When I was offered to tastes the meat I made an exceptional excuse and quite a few of us did not take part in the first sacrifice.

186.   On the second hunt, the hunters and their guides did not return until late that Saturday evening. I was holding out on my bunk when I heard a commotion, and rejoicing shouts. When I came out through the door of the camp I saw two men lifting the carcase of the black animal carrying it away behind the camp near

to where those unused ladder lays. There they were proving the concept that wild boars and armadillos lives in the everglades. They found something else to be elated about as much they have found wild yams that they dug and carried back from their hunt.

187.   As adult behaviour rise from the gain, no one but those who goes on this hunt was able to get near to the carcase. They scraped the black hairs from the boar to reveal a white underlay as they busily thrown the hot water on the hanged up carcase to help the removal of the hair easily. I stood a little distant watching them laughing and stretching the details traces of their escapade. The wild pig the day before was roaming in its habitat never dream that today it would be stringed up having nothing to say and with human adults gathering to eat its flesh.

188.   As a result of my reasoning when I was offered the meat of the pig I could not take it over from the hand that was stretching it to me. The meat was too freshly looking, but about another three days Britain had cooked the meat and ask me to taste it and I realise that it had given the men some saving not much from purchasing meat from the shop. Britain too was fast running out of purchasing power so he would have the chance to avoid purchase meat for a week or so. And if the men goes hunting again during that time successfully may be even I would participate in the sacrifice of the wild boar and take part in getting some of the meat instead of purchasing it from the shops.

189.   Nonetheless, speculation had it that wild animals around the area may be contaminated and should avoid eating after some time past. Although it did not reduce the hunting glamour. It would be carefully concealed just in case someone becomes contaminated from eating the meat of the wild animals that were caught. Then it was contemplate whether the already meat should be dump, just in case something developed and it was true and the authorities could raid the camp if somebody becomes sick after eating. Then by way of discussion we come to a measuring point that say, that over a week those who ate the armadillo's meat and the boar's meat and they were not sick already the meat were considered to be safe.

190.   Rabbits were available too, but then it would need a large catch and often to meet the need. This was not feasible as rabbits were too small for the whole camp to share in. This idea was quickly dismissed, but individuals could go after rabbits and armadillos if they so wishes. At this discussion we were told that the supervisor had received a letter from one of the men that leave the camp a month or so ago. One of the six men write that was going to join the US arm force were all sent back home to their native island with the others too.

191.   I commence to ponder after hearing what was said. The working hours were reduced, making those of us who were not resident for the winter months become concern about ourselves. I recall Matthews saying that

he was loaded down like a donkey, and how some donkeys does work its way around when things were not going too well. They would stump and kicked and make incredible noise. We thought that we would be kept because of our willingness to join the arm force, but as that letter from back home suggests that there was no guarantee of such things happens.

192.   And further to become indenture in the arm force was as well as to be dismiss and put it out my thoughts. Although the subconscious took over my mind so much so that I could not see for what I had given up my indenture for. Since we came down to Florida nobody could say or tell us what has happen to Matthew or any of those that we had spend some time together from the north. They all disappear to somewhere to some other farmer or were sent back home to their native country. One thing for sure Matthew where ever he was I surmise that he would not be sent back home solely because of his accumulated debts owed then.

- CHAPTER -
EIGHTEEN

193.   And since his Matthew's family life home remains zero he did not have anyone to pine after, send money home to nor bothered. I did not inquire whether he leave a girl friend, but he did not seem really bother one way or the other nor at all. The man was beaten by JG and to the pulp, if the story he told were truthful, and there was no reason not to believe that he was not telling the truth, and then he was a lonely man. Even make it worse was that he was believed to be a communist sympathiser that make his colleagues avoided him for all the more so.

194.   Even as I contemplate about Julie Rose and about that dress I promised her, if it had not sold by now she would have grown out of it. But then I probably bought her another of the same design with different material and now that I had my black suit to go with her dress. Or now in my suit of wrangler or levy which I bought from Youngstown in Ohio. Even if I leave the United State broke I had accumulate a few things, I knew that a few hundred dollars compulsory saving that save form me would be coming after a month or so when landed back in my country.

195.   The day before we had watched the wedding sermon of princes Margret to Lord Snowdon. In fact it was the highlight for two days on CBS and NBC the main news channels at the time. The Huntley and the Bindley were describing ever step and very nooks and crannies of the couple's movement. Reels and reel of documentation were being put through as aircraft

landed with these reels and got them to the broadcasting stations to keep us entertained. We were waking up to the wedding because of time difference while most probably people in the United Kingdom were at sleep or about to go to bed.

196.   In our case it remain the same as before desperate for answers to what is going to happen to us as we goes to bed and woken up not knowing what was going to happen in general. Some of the crew groups were still continued going and coming and telling tales of the day when they return. Our crew has been scaled down for few days well now and never set our feet out off the camp site. In the morning following the day of the wedding we sets up a cricket match. The ground was to run straight along the side of the camp. The bowlers distant to run has been shorten, also was the pitch, because of space.

197.   Everything were shorten even tempers were deeply control and was harness in the player aggressive hits of the ball and the illation that follows. It was probably the best thing to calm down the men in the early morning sunshine, when they should be out working in the field working and earning but instead of rising up having nothing to do. But then another risen problem that someone had hit the ball in the glass window and broken it after the match was over. This person was never identified but each of the camp residents had was to fork out a dollar each for the replacement window.

198.   These were dollars that we could ill ford and had we gone out to work probably the window would not have broken and a dollar would be earned rather spending a dollar. Although it might not purposely to throw or hit the ball in the camp glass window it was consider mischievous. The person may then even being suffers from intimidation and recrimination and would not own up. The crew that had gone to work and came back to find that they owed a dollar each were most unpleasant vocally since it was going to be docked from their pay check. They have no say about the unfairness of the payments.

199.   For days these insulting words were being thrown about for the culprit to own up, but he would not do so. The payment of a dollar seems to be in most cases of the men argument was the principle involve that the person who had done it should have own up instead of making everyone else pay for his fault. From the foregoing the men become suspicious of each other outside of those who were not at the camp when the window was broken and the time of the incident. There were growing animosities among the camp residents. They commence to make out that those who remain at the camp were lazy; good for nothing scroungers, forgetting that we have no control over the matter concerning working.

200.   Although our crew did not have any work to go to, we had to continue dress as though we would be called upon at anytime to go out to work. This was in operation from Monday to Saturday midday when the

readiness would reduce. On the Saturday one after noon the supervisor for the farmer called to see us and told us to get ready early the following Monday morning for work. The commencement of June month seems broken out with groves on groves of orange fields. The yellow fruits spread amongst the greenery and rows stretch for miles into the distance. They were low trees that the fruits could be picked without any kind of ladder needed. There were boxes dropped along each rows to hold the amount suspected gain from each tree.

201.   On the face of our crew including myself were ecstatic about earning some lively dollars at last. First time since leaving the apple orchard we have seen fruits bearing as though they were saying to us, 'come get us if you can,' which we did. We pluck them from their branches and filled the boxes. Within a short time the first truck loaded and gone waiting for next to be loaded and soon they were queuing up, with those that were bringing the boxes and taking away fruits boxes.

- CHAPTER -
NINETEEN

202.   When we got back to camp in the evenings laughter sprung up amongst our crew and behaving as though we had won the sweep stake. No longer were we caged in mind about our future again. Those groves we were told was where those men that had been sent home should be, but the crops were not ready so the farmer sent them directly to the Miami airport and straight home instead after a few days had past. Britain and I might not able to recoup our losses but we may and can put back a few dollars and commence to rebuild our pile.

203.   This could be the last push for the restoration of our dignity in respect of the punt. Although Britain had owed a few dollars more than I, this push could see both of us paid off McDonald and clear Uncle Sam debt. Bearing in mind and recalling Matthew's counsel although the negative side of it, was beyond our control we decided to get on with picking the fruits and settle for the consequences. We might as well benefited from the residue after payments has been deducted and go flat out. If it so be, so be it. Considering that we would return to our island not just with a few wrangler or levy in our case but also with a few dollars in our pocket.

204.   Britain may have still in mind to purchase my suit, but the push was too new to approach him on this matter just yet. He had a few more things he would like to take back home and mention that he hardly bought anything nice for his girl friend Mavis. I did not buy anything for my Girl Julie Rose either, since I hope and

have it in mind that we could go down to princess street and collar that ballerina dress when I got back for her. I could see her now in that dress. I could not see myself in a black suit walking about unless it was a funeral or something other than a function in a hot country. So if Britain wanted to buy it he would be welcome with the exception of some additional dollars for the cut.

205.   Seasonally the groves we were picking in the instant were the last of the crops. The men were already selected for winter moulding and cleaning the roots of the young trees and taking care of the groves. None of us from our crew as far as I was concern heard of anyone being selected as yet to spend the winter in Florida. Beside the rumour was that it was cheap labour during the winter months and carries lots of hazardous chemicals to work with. This was not hard for me to handle, since I been handling kerosene and other cleaning liquids that could not leave my nostrils for a while. And even though I am now away from the sump smells going ten and half months anywhere under God's creation that fluid used I could still smell it.

206.   Nonetheless, I short myself from that sort of agro an consider if I got the chance I would refuse the offer if it had given to me, and then I could got out of it and go back home with a few dollars in my pocket on the rock. The motivating factor for my part is getting back to my basic interest to be an indenture mechanic. A trade. Ten and half months I have not breathed any air from the Caribbean except those spread out from the gulf. I

have not seen a Caribbean girl walking and twisting as she moves.

207.   Ten and half months maybe a little bit more than that I have not gone to the cinema, and lately I was getting smirched by television programmes coming out of Orlando and elsewhere around the continent. I was not quite sure how I would behave having a few dollars in my packet and some more to come. I am not even sure about Barbara when I got back she was going to want me. See, many girls avoid men with money however little. Barbara and I never discuss these features of us living together or having money earned from outside of my trade and what Mr Jiles paid me at the weekends. Any tips coming from the customers when I watered and check their oil and wiped down their mirror with the soft cleaning cloth I had in my pocket had been mine.

208.   There were many things that become border line as my life spiral into manhood. It was almost leaving me behind. My mind has been bombarding myself with features that should not be thinking of so regularly. The point of living with a girl without marring her was battering my mind. It was the think my mother and guardian would shudder about for a fact and when I came back to camp tired and should have gone to bed and sleep tiredly. It woke me up to chastise me so that in the morning I would awoken tired as though have not gone to bed the whole night through.

SELLING MY LAST SUIT

209.   Then it was this thing of my mother constantly saying in my presence about marrying a nice girl. Although she had seen Julie Rose once or twice with me together she might not know how far our relationship has developed. But knowing my mum she might by now being well aware of the situation far ahead of me little covertness. They would be looking and listening for whispers about marriage as soon they knew I was back on the island. Seem in my mind they already worked out plans and if they had not then it would continue as normal. But things in the juvenile mind have never been normal at all.

210.   Following the years of growing up and my mother and guardian pumping their experience including others like family and friends into me. Not forgetting Matthew with his last little bit. My body and soul were spiralling out of control and with the mind activated like a volcano it was hard to tell where it was going too, and where it would end with this driven engine attached to my body somewhere. Now that we had two weeks of hard working. Picking fruits from the trees until late in the evenings and returning early before the morning sun came out and the dried dew. It was not hard although not being told that we were on the last push.

211.   By then we did not hear anything from the US recruiters that had been selecting men to join the army as advisors to Vietnam. Six of those recruitees who left the camp earlier rumoured that they were all at Florida international waiting to board their aircraft to

their varying and respective countries in the Caribbean. In the morning when we looked at those orange trees and the grove that we worked on the previous day it look as though a hurricane passes through. Midweek of the third week we got our pay pocket for half a week payment with a little difference to the low payments we have had since we came down to Florida picking fruits.

212.   Payments were made fortnightly on Wednesday's. I calculate that a full two weeks and a little with few more dollars would be in the pay pocket on the next pay day arrival. If I landed back on the island with these dollars without deduction I reason out that I could travel to England by paying my own fare. This would not be a hard thing to do. Since it was considered that Jamaica and the other island belong to Great Brittan and so too those living on it were her subject. But I probably could return to and ask Mr Jiles if he would consider restating my apprenticeship and consider the length of time I was away as being vocational time out. I might even do little graveling in the process.

213.   At this point what would be happening to our crew was uncertain, but rumours were quite plentiful and most time they were based on those who already gone and travel through the history of the contract maker. I notice on my pay slip also that the balance was cleared and I owed zero now to Uncle Sam. Britain was talking to me about our weak stand to remain in the United States. Immediately I pass through my mind over Matthew suggestion from the outset. But I could

not come to terms with that part of his thoughts, because I did believe in paying off debts owed. It might not that Matthew would not pay off his debt, but it seems that he linger and hold back the payments that he owed. "Like the large Countries." He bemoaned.

214.   "Large countries like the United States never pay off their debts. But they can give incentives like us coming to work over here." "This bothers me." And told him about my uncle who own a little grocery shop. I heard him curse and talk disparaging of those who did not pay their debts whether on time or at all. But those who paid on time hold well with him and he speak respectful of them so that any goods they could get by mentioning their names. But Matthew holds this view and he would not pay off his debt either if he could help it. Now that I have paid off my debt I becomes a liability to Uncle Sam' while I was going through my afflicted sentence.

– CHAPTER –
TWENTY

215.   My mother has this little poem she used to tell us and it goes like this: 'speak the truth and speak it ever cast it where it will. They who hides the wrong they do. Do wrong thing still.' Never get the full grasps of it, since adults used to scorn us and hide things that they afraid we might see and talk. Like the adults I know who were milking another man's cows while the owner slept early in the mornings. This affected me since I told my mother about this man stealing from the other man's cows by milking them but she shouts at me and told me to watch my mouth. So I concluded and was convinced that adults wear double garments for the sake of staying out of trouble when it suits them and their colleagues.

216.   Why mother could not just goes up to the man and told him that I have seen him milking the man cows on several early mornings? Even though the owner complaining that his cows were not giving enough milk? "States and governments are like that. They steal, told lies, barrowed, hold onto their debts to each other and although individuals may know and told so, nobody do anything about it. Because that's how it works." Matthew told me. "The longer they hold onto not paying is the more respect and cajoling involved to get payments."

217.   "Like our little country. It'll never able to pay off its debt to other countries they owed. So they give facilities, like us the farm worker. We're helping to reduce that debt to Uncle Sam. The longer we stay with Uncle Sam the more debt we reduce for our country." "I see!" I acknowledged. Did you learn this on your first

travel?" "Fair play, they called it." He said and mourned.
"You've to be grown up to understand it."

218.   Now that I review and think about the statement
of Matthew and know that I could not hold back myself
from paying off Uncle Sam quickly although any one
saying to contrary. It was forced by indirect means of
allurement with induce incentives. But now the time
was coming where the end of the uncertainty begins to
climax and the farmer duly draws in more pickers and
shorten the time span. When we got to the field on the
third week of the push, there were crews from other
camps already in the field picking oranges. Even at that
time other trucks which we had never saw were turning
the engines and the men were dropping empties and
loading filled boxes on the opposite side of the grove.

219.   We were late getting to our grove because it was
raining early in the morning that we taught we would
not be going out for the day. But the rain had stopped
and dried up part of the morning when our camp vehicle
picks us up. The guideline was not to pick fruits when
they were wet, especially if they had been sprayed
the day or two previously. Even so the groves already
sprayed a few days before and picking the fruits were
harmless at this time and by the time we reached the
field the sun came up and dried it out almost as if no
rain had been falling. The fruits were glistening in the
sun. Then the sky was blued and the sun pitched so low
in the sky as though it could be touched by climbing a
tall ladder by human hands.

220.   We got onto our rows on which we were picking fruits that we left off the previous week end. There were still good fruits to be picked and plenty to do in this field that may last for two or three days, but not enough for the full week. Boxes were dropped at each fruit tree according to the guess yield. We lost in no time to pick up our ladder and hoist it on our shoulder and walked along the rows to the fruit tree. There upon we would commence picking the luscious fruits, and filled our side bags as quickly as we can to strip the tree of its yellow fruits and filed the boxes. A whole bag filled with orange depending on their size filled one of two apartment of the box. If it had been grapefruits the box would fill quicker than the oranges, but the payments for each box was about fifty percent lower for that of the grapefruit to the orange to compare.

221.   Just after lunch when we got back and the truck commence to load up the finish boxes. Someone shouts, "Officials on our case," "who said so?" I inquired and shout back. "Because two official black vehicle in the interval out there." One of the men from our crew replied. "See them before?" "Yep, seen them before." "What they want?" "Talking to the foreman now, one of them." "Glean anything, what they're saying?" "Too far away." "One of us goes and gets some water, linger a bit." The community now called out for the most discrete one to go for a drink since one of the men now stood aside off while the other were giving something like instructions. The high alert focus was put immediately

in any seeming alteration that would disrupt our being pounce upon by discrete officials.

222.   All in our crew already pay off Uncle Sam and was just work and paying for our food and shelter. Anything earn now would be savings and even though it was not has been the earning up north a few more dollars could be securely added to our pile. My pile too. The only damaging result would be for us to earn a bit and then stop at the camp as before having nothing to do and spending out that which we have just earned. When the community leader Douglas, returns he asked another about how soon we could get the liaison officer. Although in any emergency and belief he would be with us within a short while none emergency would take him days to see us probably even longer.

223.   I surmised then that something was afoot and Douglas the community leader bought back a cylinder of drinking water sweating as much water in perspiration. He was quick to put us at ease, promising that he got the liaison officers telephone and would try to sort out uncertainty with him from what he had glean. But then Wiley who had been keeping a low profile for a while demand to know what the two men were saying to the foreman. The report was patchy and need ciphering to be made clear. Douglas was holding back from what he heard to tell the men so. Even if he had some knowledge of what the officials were up to, he reserves his findings because he did not want to be in trouble.

224. Although latter on he would be in trouble whether he likes it or not he was in the deep. The more he seems to explain that he heard only few words it was not enough to form a truthful opinion on the matter. Most of us then alter our views and suspect Douglas' straight forwardness and began to view him as a spy that was not so much a good one at that. Posing that the gleaning he kept only for himself and revealing only what he wants to. The hints he had given were like in words form like: "Michigan, New York, winter months and going home swiftly after this."

225. "Before the week is out something's going to happen to us." I told them and walked off and return to picking the oranges. By then the two black cars had gone and only the dust rising from the dusty road they were travelling on in the distant. Where the eyes could see from the pitch on the ladder. One of the trucks too was travelling on the same direction dusty road with boxes of loaded oranges going to the pulping factory some distant away at Mims. Leaving us in quandary peddling the fact from the fiction and bottoming out the obstacle from fact. Surely there must be some fact about even if in the unlikely event that someone could give us some calcification of our suspicion. Nobody was in any mode to believe anybody whatsoever may be pondering. However the fact remains that we did not know what was going on. It would be or sound from our crew or to alleviate the suspected result that we were out and were going home. We decided that something was

going on but could not further add any truthfulness to the outcome one way or the other.

226.   I was bobbing and wavering whether I should descend into my spiritual self to find out what was happening. "When you're in doubt. You pray my son. Get down on them knees and do it." Mother would console and pointed to my knees by her index. My engine was running low on doubts of the future happening and a need for outside lubricant was obvious. We had just commenced our little pile of putting back a few dollars onto the existing roll. Turning into the middle of the third week continuously working this field could not sustain another week of the aggressive picking of fruits. There were mostly young men hurrying to pick and filled more boxes in our crew. Then from those boxes mean more dollars yield. I was still the youngest in this crew and could stand up to anything better of the best.

227.   My youthfulness and a lack of having sex since we leave Ohio some months ago meant that I had enough work to alleviate the stress of not having girls around for that purpose. And then in the formation of information that needed to be cipher and how much dollars if I return home I need to live on. Unfortunately for me, I now grown accustom to living with television and having food daily to eat and listening to music on my own radio that was not affordable for me at apprentice school. People back home always look upon a traveller to be rich, and especially travelling to Uncle Sam's country would be a boon for those not experience to believe it to be so.

– CHAPTER –
TWENTY ONE

228.   It had been just over eleven months now since I left the island and while Florida seems to be having the same ambient as Jamaica has, the culture has been slightly different and varied in cultural analysis of the same spec. The foreman called for the end of the day working and we pack our ladder onto the side of the panel truck that would take us back to the camp at Mims. Douglas asked the foreman to explain what those officials were about before we mounted onto the truck. "O." He replied. "Some of you boys will be stopping with us for the winter, but not all of you will be. Others may be going home. You will be told who is going home and who will be stopping before the weekends out. Can't be sure which of you will be stopping here for the winter months."

229.   "It's alright for you all. When you get back home." As we mounted onto the panel truck I gestured to no one particularly in words. Going back home with those dollars might be adequate for some, but for me there were probably trouble in store more than I could feasible handle. Wiley was sure that he would be one of the first on the list to go home. But he had reservation that JG if he was around to be told that he was on his way home would leave quietly. Britain remain subdue himself and since we started driving back to the camp he seem to be deep in concentration. But everybody was contemplating of the outcome. Although two of the men knew that they would be on the list of those who were going to spend winter in Florida such as Douglas who most certainly would remain.

230.   They too were not sure but as they spent the last wintering in Florida it was presumed that they were. It depending on good behaviour and unless they had been checked out and were not up to speed in their first year then. There had been lively humorous discussion returning to the camp even though we were delay for sometime because of a low loader vehicle carrying large missile parts to the cape. It was travelling probably not more than a couple of miles per hour. The issue of JG once again held high on the floor and engender issues that characterised his knowledge of when men would be returning home. Since he well know about the seasonal crops and when the farm workers might be on his way home.

231.   And as JG was more or less a step ahead of his contemporaries it was not very often that a surprise could be sprung on him during his escapade. There was no called for any action was to be taken against JG for his overhaul cunning behaviour and activities, and sometime conceitedness. As pointed out and as the detail goes about JG could be from any of the genders taking advantage of the capability endowed a specific situation. JG also operates from any strata, and mostly active in the higher echelon of society. But then he had no choice and can chose the lowest part to operate from. It did not matter to him while, and so long as he is scoring against another human been.

232.   A few of them was admitting that they too had operates in JG shoes and the reason being the

opportunity present itself that could not be forfeited. I listen to the men detailing and giving samples of their audios effort a times to bring their intention to play and fruition. I did not enter into the discussion, since I had no experience to relate. As the low loader branches off leading to the cape, our engine revered and speeded to take us back to the camp the humorous mood swings away from JG conquest and I could hardly hear what was being said owing to the roaring and noise of the vehicle.

233.　On Wednesday although we went to the grove late more fruits were picked per hour than the other full days. After the truck that took us back to the camp had driven off and we went inside. There were two letters on my bunk. One was from Julie Rose and the other writing I could not identify unless it was open. But I took them both, smell the identify one and pushed into my back pocket and hide the unidentified one under the pillow. Then I went into the kitchen to do some cooking with the other men that had just came in. The conversation around JG elicits the poking of fun from the mail some of the men were reading. Conversely those who did not have any mail were bemoaned that their female were too busy looking about JG to take up a pen and write.

234.　I felt though that keeping my letter from my girl confidentially would avoid getting into any fun poking humour. Relentless effort was afoot to read interpreted and replace words over the shoulder of the ones who had opened their letters and having quick glances. Although JG might not have been evolved the over shoulder reader would say so and for a while I thought that soon there would be confrontation along the hot stove in one of the columns. It was time for the camp supervisor who might have heard something else and differently came in the kitchen and steps in to quiet the men down who seems were boiling as the pots were.

235.   The confrontation however spilled over in the yard latter on in the evening when another one of the men had taken issues against the other for insulting his girl. By the time I understand that a scrap was outside. It was over quite quickly when I got there but I was in time to see both men were boiling with anger and had to be held back several time from the clash. None of the men were from our crew so any anger might be fought out on the other crew's path since they belong to one of the same.

236.   After the small punch up outside I went inside and pull out the letter from my girl that was securely read and put under tight security and check regularly. Although I did not consider JG a treat, the rumour about him had been so strong that it influences my rethinking without being anxious or jealous about him and his antics. I then open the other letter that seems written in a hurry. It was from Matthew. I could not hold back from shouting, 'Matthew writes. Matthew writes!' 'O, Matthew.' Britain shouted back. 'What he's saying now?' Wiley inquired. 'He's spending winter in

Florida and hopefully will be shipped back up north for summer.' 'Uncle Sam may have to send him home in shackles.' 'Max is three years.' 'He'll get six, if they allow it.' 'He'll get it, maybe forever.'

237.   'Said to say hello to you all. And sorry that he did not get chance to say goodbye. 'Is he alright?' 'Must be. Uncle Sam takes him healthy so they must keep him as the original product until he landed back on the rock. ' 'It's a pity he his son won't acknowledge him.' 'He wishes us all well and hoping that we got the chance to stay over in Florida for the winter.' The camp supervisor came in and was listening and told us that those from that camp will be going to Apple in New York come spring summer months. 'Good catch for your friend.' He told us. 'The letter ends with, Good luck with no forwarding address.' I told them without they read the letter themselves.

238.   Early morning the following day we got ready to face the day and contemplating the outcome of the day in front of us. I went into the kitchen to make a pack lunch but when I finish doing it by then the truck would arrive and we would be ready to go onto the field, but it did not come. All twenty of us linger about listening keenly to hear the roaring of the Bedford engine and the crushing on the gravel as the tyres pulps in the distant coming. Several time someone make announcements that they could hear the engine of the vehicle revving and certain that it was coming. But it was not to be. No one at that time given views of anything else beside

the lateness of the vehicle with the lunch carrier pack holding bobbing up and down in their hands. By then those other crews two of them had been picked up and wisps away an hour or so ago.

- CHAPTER -
TWENTY TWO

239.   From early days I had invested in one of the small army like shoulder bag which I used to carry my pack lunch since I came down to Florida. It was on my shoulder reminisce like I was back to school each morning only this was in more adults form. Besides we would be walking to a structure our school instead of waiting around in a yard listening for a vehicle that would not be coming. Those ladder packed on top of one another were still lying there alongside the camp with growing weeds sprouting out from between each steps.

240.   The men that were using them had long been gone. Some of them were back on their home soil or they could be back in United States on the same farm runs. Nobody heard of what happen to the individuals beside the one letter the supervisor got from one of those who had been sent back home. Those detail were very scarce although some of them were check out to join the US army as advisors in Vietnam. I too was a part of that selection but at the moment I presume things was not going accordingly. Might somebody drop a spanner in the job-for recruitment of farmer worker to be supervisors in the US army?

241.   I could not say or determined the outcome, but that has dripped down in my mind that adults could be meddlesome and interfere into the running of a juvenile life. Not old enough to be an adult and even considered being silly and always not functioning rightly. This I consider that adults may covertly meddle and uses the

law to ender. "Don't live long enough-don't have enough experience-don't see the world as it is-need to go back to his mum's breast-no say 'till you're twenty one, boy." Even now as I stood leaning against the padlock ladders and pondering, that if I return to the island I still could not take part in nothing other than the youthful prank as sets out in the law of the land.

242.   Sometime after an hour passed there was a car driven chastely past the camp with a couple of men inside. Douglas who assumes he would be staying there for the winter was sure that one of the men in the vehicle was our liaison officer. 'If he is, why did he past?' 'If that is him, it means that someone reported the scrap outside last night. It meant trouble.' 'None from our crew was involved.' Someone stated. 'We know that. The liaison officer doesn't come along unless he brings bad news or someone report the fight or something else and he come to sort it out.' Douglas reiterated.

243.   Soon following the debate with the uncertainty partly concludes the car that had just past return and pulled up calmly in the dusty mall yard. Florida had been class as segregated states, but an exception must have been waved within its legal framework between employer and their employee. But also we were not American but British subject and on contract to work in the United States. Therefore, we were class as British boys from north to south anywhere we go there was a liaison officers place there or nearby to sort indifferences or trouble. The car doors did not open immediately and

delayed as though they were waiting for something to happen or somebody else to come along.

244.   Not long there was another car like the same with two men pulled up alongside the other car and wasted no time in getting out of their vehicle. The others from the first car came out too and they greeted each other. They were not as friends but seem to be colleagues that discuss things from their varying departments to get thing done. Then they walked back out onto the dusty chalk like road and divided themselves into twos walking along and grumbling exchange. Probably they were discussing about who would be chosen to tell us the bad or the good news.

245.   My natural inclination then was to go on start packing, but was uncertain of the outcome. The foreman had told our crew that a decision would be made before the weekend. And we already knew that we were only saved from not going home because these groves fruits were not fully mature. The men who had been sent their too early, they were sent home and now we were coming to the end of reaping of those groves our homeward bound must be on the card at that. Now that the uncertainty becoming it would be a disappointment if the result was different from what I had in mind to be sent home.

246.   The men stood in the shade of the upcoming and warm sunshine exchanging and debating. They were too far away for us to hear a whisper but things were afoot. I wondered why they did not have their

meetings before arriving instead of holding it outside the camp site. The law of the states may have prohibited the commune under one roof by the different race and this was the way they have to do it. Again they walked back to their respected vehicle leaving the door ajar getting some papers from their folder showing each other their directives of confirmation by pointing and reading the information.

247.   We were the piggy in the middle and we come to know it, from their behaviour. When they agreed it seems the liaison officer ask Douglas to call the camp supervisor who was at one of the netted window looking out. The camp supervisor would clean and keep the camp tidy always and even to made up the bedding when we gone out to work. Only things he would not do were the washing and cooking for us which we had to do for ourselves. It was training like in the army or the scouts for all of us men since many of us did not know how to cook and feed ourselves. To wash our clothes and getting used to ironing them was a chore. Our working cloths and smalls we would wash and since there were no women to chastise and see us, we keep the official laundries for those that we ware on the weekends.

248.   The supervisor came out and spoken to the liaison officer and went back through the mosquito netted door for a short while he return and call the men inside the camp. We were left outside debating what these men were up to and what it was about, but as for me I wanted to catalogue this to my experience collections. Then the

supervisors came out and told us about the meeting that would be held in the canteen for all of us to attend. They marched to the canteen and we were told to sit down by the liaison officer. By then one of the truck that had gone out with pickers earlier returned with the men who came straight to the canteen as well. They too were told to take a seat by the officers.

249.   "Those of you from both crews. Listen for your name. Those who hear their names call will be staying with their company. The others will be going home immediately. Leaving for the airport early tomorrow morning. A bus will come for you to take you to the Miami International. There you will be put on a flight back to your respective country. " following straight away the liaison officer talk one of the other men stood up and began to call the names out. It was a few names like, 'Britain, Bruce, Cole, Douglas, James, and Pusey. As you know these are the men that will be staying over. Thank you for your cooperation.'

250.   The other man introduces himself when he got up to speak. I glance around and saw those who had been chosen to stop over they were grinning like a top cat seeing cheese for the first time. Only six from the forty four of us were stopping over and thirty eight would be catching the bus for the airport the following morning. I was not disappointed even though I got issues. But then I could probably cope with them more than the uncertainty at the minute of staying over and staring down to become broke in the face which I almost did.

251.   "So, here come Britain Vietnam and out go Page back on the rock." I said in gesture. But the liaison officer looked at me with a surprise look as to say, 'Who told you anybody was going anywhere.' 'Good god.' Wiley shout. 'It hardly worth it, just as we were about to make a few dollars. The field not finish picking?' The man who stood up to tell us about our payments then asks for calmness while we listen. But quite a few of the men who had flown directly to pick citrus may have had just those few weeks of good pickings. Now they would be going home with little and I recall what Mr Jiles had told me, that of some men returning, 'with only large suitcases with nothing in them.'

252.   Wiley argued with a few of the other men asking questions that none of the four men including the liaison officers could answer. They had a job to do and that job was to tell us that the contract had simply completed. That we were engaging to do and they were there to ensure to see us out the country as soon as it could be done. The following morning was the soonest. I leave the men in counter arguing in the canteen and went to over look my suitcase. I know that Britain would be interested in buying my suit and I was going to give him the first refusal. I met him coming in through the door. "I'm selling the suit, and since you're staying you can afford it now and you've always wanted it to buy." "How much? "120 dollars cash." "How much did you pay for it?" "Commodity grows in value."

- CHAPTER -
TWENTY THREE

253.   "Give you 115 dollars." "Let's split the five and it's yours." Britain went away for a little while I could hear the sound from his trunk opening and close. I stood there with my suit that I know within a short while it would not belong to me anymore and the big world for me was getting bigger and more complex even though a still have little over a year when I would hit being twenty one years. I handed Britain the suit as it was. He pushed in my right hand one hundred twenty dollars. I return him two dollars and fifty cents and handover his goods. It was a sale I regretted but it had to be done. Britain handed me a little parcel after he took his product from my hand I did not open it. I glanced at him without staring him in the face, 'I hope, he dare not given me one of those cheap present he was bartering for one day when we went shopping,' I mumbled to myself........

254.   Early the following morning the owner came to see us before we got onto the coach to make our way to Miami International. He gave me the envelope that contains all the money due and asked whether I would like to return to the United States of America. I told him, 'yes I would like to return,' he didn't hesitate, 'which I'll do for you Page.' 'Thank you,' I replied and walked away onto the coach followed by the others. All thirty eight of us including some from our crew making up the number of us that were on the coach. Uncle Sam paid us up and only the outstanding balance would be our security savings that were taken from us during our working for him.

255. A month hence we would be picking up the first of the payment in our country of origin covering the bigger share of the amount firstly. It was not stipulate whether it would be by date or would it be the following month from the date when we landed. Although nobody could certain what that shares would be either. This could open to questionable view of the amount to be paid. Since every dollar in the kitty Uncle Sam would contribute some percentage towards the accumulation the farm workers earned. But on that point the amount gotten by the farm worker could be reduce and raided by the government of origin and form a big catch for them too. The coach started to move away from Mims camp and soon the wave from the remainders lasted for just awhile. I sat down but was lonely, thinking and asking about-what has change?

256. I could not have gotten more out of experience had he attended university of higher learning from the practicality point of this travel that I had gained. Eleven months and two days put together my short span of life lived of more than the six thousands eight hundred days that I have lived and make up for them. The coach now leaves the dusty and misty road and hit on the highway to the Miami International and since along it was more or less Britain and I travelling from Jamaica. Considering that he was alone now and have to make new friends of the older men who responsible to teach him the knocks and hooks. He probably discusses minor thing but not his deep boy's things and thinking with them as he would with me.

257.   Soon I would be home and back on our rock as well known by the farm workers. Hard and unforgiving but soothe the pain with the continuous sunshine, and not as glamorous as then known rock of Gibraltar of Mediterranean, but still called the rock for those who suffer on it. All my friends that I have made now left and pull apart like threads from old garments. We might never see each other again. Even if we had the time and occasion might be different or insufficient comparing to the length of time spend together during this travel. It was an awesome experience and far more than so returning home, which has some raised questions and issues some of which I am about to face shortly before the day closed. I have two homes that I could go to for sure, that of my guardians and the other my mother. Now that I remain still a juvenile I considered that if anything happen to the contrary I could rent an apartment and return to the state eleven months previously. Although I was not responsible to pay that rent before, now I would be paying it if I should encounter problem of the sort I envisage.

258.   I knew that my mother would haughtily welcomes me back with some reservation and even different from my guardians who may have change towards my ungratefulness, even though it was not strictly so intentionally. They might allow me to stay only for a short period considering that I am an earner with travelling experience. Julie Rose have grown up too so she might have intentionally want us to informed

her mother and family about us getting together and my family also which deem they may suggest some sort of marriage arrangement. But all of this was outside what I wanted to do in the sense that I would like to be indenture before I get to the twenty one of none return. Those months were rolling by and the time left has been reduce and once I had time but I would be shortly running out of it. Days were rolling upon it, and streams of fermentation had taken me just over ten minutes to collectively sum up my present future views of things coming.

259.   By the time I regain about my present that coach was well on its way clearing the Mims district and all that had left behind was just memory. The man that sat beside me who I have not spoken to since we left out probably was thinking the same, because all I could hear was the growling of the engine, the tyres crushing the road underneath upon the asphalt and other vehicles that were passing and some time horning. It was speeding to get us to the airport assuredly as he could do so quickly. Gaining on myself I open the discussion and ask the man sat by me to express some views. He was from another crew so we have not much in common before, but now we were bonded together in a seat on a bus going home so it was time I consider that we make acquaintances and I fired the first of the many shots. "First time travel?" "Second time for me." "So you well know the running?" "I was up here last year to the orange, first time." "By the way my name's Page, what's

yours again?" He stretched out his right hand across and met mine. "Ankle mine." Ankle was talkative as much even though I picked up straight away that he was not comfortable owing from the trembling coming through his voice box unregulated.

260.　Soon everybody were talking and exchanging thoughts from a mumbling that arisen to a full voice over conversation qualities. I was listening to audios and the mumbling coming from far down the coach as it sped through the villages attach nearest to the highway. "Which of the saint you're from" I asked Ankle. This was to keep the momentum going and also to listen for any mention of the JG argumentation we had some months previously on our journey when coming to the south. "Saint Thomas." He replied coldly. "Me, I'm from Saint Catherine." "Where you hang people, Spanish town." He mentioned laughingly but seems to be serious about his remarks. "Wouldn't go down that road, but yes bad men hang there." "Innocent hangs there too." "Possible." "What you're going to do about the innocent?" "Me? Have nothing to do with that sort of thing. Have anybody hang there?"

261.　"No, not that I know about, but England hang a lot of innocent men there. Nobody knows how many." "Could be." "That's for sure, and nobody could stop them from doing so-even god couldn't, they would kill god too if they could catch him." "You think?" "Not if I think so-I know so, they would, don't you know?" "Yes, yes" I replied. "I do know so." Shortly Henderson who was talking to his partner that sat with him on the opposite seat asked about Joe Grind. "What would they say if I go home and catch Joe Grind with my wife and kill him?" "Fought!" Ankle jested. "A whole lot of men want to do away with that feller, even me." "That guy eats your food, take your woman and if you got children he takes the lot." Henderson complimented the infamous character.

262.   "I heard that it could be a woman, can she do as much damage as man can?" I argued and asked. "No." Ankle replied laughingly. "In our case he's not a woman we're talking about here, it's a feller. For us is a feller, a guy. It's a man." "Sure." I jested. "He must have some reason to do what he's doing?" "No, sir, he's a wrecker of life." A voice lifted from a little distance down the coach creaked out. "This man is pushing the vehicle to get us there in a hurry, but we might be there from when we got there up to two, three days at the airport." Ankle noted. "We're not the only farm workers going home now-you know that? There's hundreds of streaming humans there waiting for flights to go home." Henderson states. "They don't feed you well there at all, pittance of food."

263.   "You." Henderson looked at me with his plucked eyes said. "You're going to starve if they don't send you off quickly." "Could buy some food." I countered "They don't let you wonder around the airport, afraid you might slip contract." Ankle agreeing with that statement Henderson makes. "Boy, they caged you

and sets up strong security there. This is the hardest part, going home; they punish your box side here, for good." "Bearing in mind, sometime they could of riots there if they're not careful. That's why all the security." That creaking voice stated. "Cracks appear all over the place when the men want to get home, and waiting at airport all day and night not knowing when they'll leave for home. They make the men spend off some of their money too."

264. "That's where the cracks start for definite. They'll hold onto you there until you spend some of the dollars you have on you." Henderson continued. "It's easy for them to know how much dollars we have on us, leaving the country with." "How could they know that?" I asked suspicious of the inclined level the discussion spiralling and wangling upwards into. Then I recalling the time when we first came down to Florida with piles from the north and soon men commence to hunted armadillos and wild boars to suffice and adjust to save a few dollars. It was not the ultimate reason but alternative prospect that if things do turn nastier and for the sake of surviving until the fruits were ready to be reaped.

265. I return back to the discussion even though I conclude that this must be so and agreeing with the travelled men on what they were stating. It was obvious that they might have had gutful of experience that I would wanted to collect as much since mine extended only to my travelled to the United State, and to a few

of the states within. Only I find myself not gravitating to listening only but I also wanted to purge the ongoing for factual experience so that I could relates to in the coming situation I soon find myself in as well. But by the time I returned to the discussion there were some heavy weights entered with audible vocals mentoring and countering suggestive feature of their agonised experience.

266. "Even if you should spend off all your earned dollars." One from the heavyweights continued. "Your last pay check tells them a calculated fact. And say within us we have around twenty thousand dollars. You might not leave that airport until some of those dollars return by spending some of it." "Then you know that before-don't you?" Ankle turns to me and asked. "Didn't know the half of it." I replied. "After all is our money." "Maybe so." Henderson quibbles. "This is the USA, their almighty dollars belongs to them, and if you're hungry and have the money in your pocket-are you going to starve?" "Got a little to keep me, if that should happen for a while." I inserted.

- CHAPTER -
TWENTY FOUR

267. Every moment spent with these men and hear them speak from one think to another make intrigued listening. Sometimes their voice rose to a high pitch that can become scary for a stranger that might conclude that, 'a fight is going to break out shortly,' but this wasn't so. The atmosphere combine with laughter after a point is made reduce any cord for injury to be followed. But the gaff that had been back at the camp some time ago was caused by a vengeful antagonist remarks made about the family, and beside to capitalised on the remarks which feature JG, infamously.

268. This was out of order with the many concluding and span some varmint remarks that even now refer slightly to the ultimate were to break the remarked back. Even when so reason to gave some solace while our environment was being change from a moment to another, and being so that just before the coach hit the airport perimeter it commence to rain within the sunshine. "Rain is tumbling down." Shouts some as though we all could not see or hear the droplets. "Its rainbow weather this is." While some stare out the windows to see who would firstly spotted the rainbow that was presumably was somewhere around in the sky. The rain lasted as long until we got to the terminal and disembarked.

269. We were lead into a sort of bunker, and soon we were joined as was the theory, by hundreds of men like a busy market place. I looked around to glance at the rest of the family. Some were leaning against post. Some were sitting down on boxes while others were slowly

unintentionally moving about. Some were inhaling the cigarette slowly and as long as they could hold the smoke within their breath, then they would puffed it out in huge blanket, and go back to take the same deep inhaling that was done previously. It had shown some sort of desperation on the face of these men.

270.   I moved along to look around, although by now I had lost the sight of most of those men that I travelled together with and I made no effort to look about for my case that travelled on the bus with me. Soon though a person came shouting about the passenger that had just came to go and fetch their luggage from the coach. All the cases and trunks were packed in a compartment and we had to go and sort them out individually. By then the coach had gone away not to be seen again. It was not far off that I saw my trunk almost put aside as though somebody selected and carefully put it there where I could find it easily.

271.   I took my trunk and moved back into the main building. A little spot near where another man was sitting on his trunk where I put mine. It was Harriett who we travelled from Wisconsin to Ohio and now we were back together again. This was even more so of a friend and a colleague that lay the first contact with, like this first layer of our travelled experience. We would be catching up on the missing months. Harriett and I were not as close as Britain and me, but this time it was different, because Britain would now be replaced, as a missing friend.

272.   Harriett introduce me to another friend he called, 'Flymug' with a wide grin so much so that I enquire whether this was a real name of his friend and if not what would be the explanation for this name. "Because my name is an easy one to remember." Flymug explained. "Those boys from the camp gave me it." "And you like it?" I asked grinning as much, but then I surmised that there might be a reason for this man to like this pseudo name. "Yes." He replied. "That dam fly, flying aground my mug one morning. I try to box it away and my mug goes flying so goes my name as Flymug." I paused for a moment and looked at the man and he was happy. By then some others have joined in the laughter. Then I realised that somehow anyone could be a comedian having a captive audience.

273.   There was not enough material to keep this audience happy for long. Much more it would have to be good material to awaken some of the more hard case to be given even a grin much more and audible laughter for any given time. From time to time someone would crack an internal joke somewhere in the distant which filtered down to us who could not hear or even understand the joke but we laughed as much. This was to pass the time as we await our aircraft to arrive. It was coming into midday, and from the windows we could see that the skies were black and the sun was not shining as it were when we arrived. "Only one plane." Someone shouts. "Only one aeroplane, so we have to wait until it returns again and again."

274.   "How long that'll take?" Another person asked. "Anybody guess." I was told about the difficulties that may encounter at the airport when I ask Harriett whether he was aware of it. But he did not and neither was Flymug. Since it was like me, it was our first travel and none of us was told about the difficulties. It seems officially and even at that moment it would assume that there had been no specifics. And if any specified knowledge about it was scarcely informed for us and terms we understood. Presumably, this was picked up from the older traveller as a 'pass-me-down and word of mouth' that become officially the norm.

275.   But some would not get the normal treatment unless they continue to prick their ears for information and so some would leave out. "We're here from yesterday evening." Flymug commented. "And when we came here there were hundreds of men about the same amount that is here now. They've been flying in and out all day and it doesn't look as though they're reducing the amount." "How about dinner and lunch?" I asked. "That!" Harriett then answered. "I think they might bring us here to starve us or let us spend the money. Just a little pack lunch, couldn't feed a rat." "We eat biscuits from yesterday until we fed up of eating it, tell you the truth."

276.   "Where you sleep, then?" I asked. "On your trunk or you can go inside there. Men in there still sleeping now." Flymug move off and beckon with his hands that I should followed him that he could show me where

the men were sleeping. He pulled back the sliding door and certainly men were sleeping on the floor, on their trunk or on top of their suitcases as though there were no daylight hours. There were a few men stoop down in the corner playing cards for money noiselessly. I glance around to see if there was anyone I might recognise hurriedly, but I could not be certain of anyone even onto those who were sleeping.

277.   "Those." I concluded that those asleep were comfortable. "Tiredness makes men sleep and that just what they're doing." Flymug moved off and I went back with him where we were previously, at our suitcases and trunks. By then another man lean against my trunks as though he wanted to sit down and used it for a seat, but I was in time to ask him not to do so. He was looking as though he recognised me, and I too but 'where' I pondered. It was Harriett that asked. "Don't you remember him Page-we were at Wisconsin together." "O, yes now I know where." "You don't remember me?" He asked placidly. "I show you to your bunk when you first arrived at Foxlake."

278.   "Yes, yes I remember you now." Flymug pulled out a pack of camel cigarette that he handed it around. I did not smoke camel and pulled out my full strength capstan. I know that Harriett did not smoke capstan, but instead he smoke chesterfield which he pulls out too and offered a cigarette to the other man which he took lingeringly. Often I smoke capstan full strength as from Matthews time which he had teaches me to

smoke. I believe then that anywhere I saw Matthew we would have a social smoking from the capstan brand. I would watched him after lighted up took that deep pull to his lungs and keep the smoking inhaling in such a long-time it would be coming through his ears. But it never did come out visually and often wondered what has happen to that smoke he inhale.

279. "A batch of us went to New York, at apple." The man told us. "Any good over there?" "Yea" he replied and took another sharp pull into his lungs from the camel that he took from Flymug pack. "Yea, man-it was good over there. Plenty women and plenty dollars. Good bearing fruit." He widen out his two hands showing how large the apples were. It was not long for the idle men commence to tell of their capture with haughtily laughter and joined by some older men too who readily and willing to pass the time off with chatter. Nobody there seem to responsible even to tell us when we would be leaving the port or what else should happen and soon the confusion of leaving our hope becomes debatable. I usually learn to put a time span on things to happen with an overhaul longer time duration for it.

280. This time the length of time was for three days for going home to happen. Any time span earlier would be satisfactory even though the treatment within that time may be different in that it might caused some problems even hidden that was not foresaw in the immediate or present. Looking through the windows the rain was still continuously pouring down and becomes damp

inside where we were as other men arrived in the pack departure bay. They were scurrying to find a place to park their cases that were hardly available as foot space reduced in view of the men just arrived.

– CHAPTER –
TWENTY FIVE

281.   It was not long then things commence to move a bit when the liaison officers arrived with some other men. They stood on the upper floor of the building just a little way from the main stairs looking over the balcony almost directly over where we stood on the ground floor base. There was security men in the form of attendant stood at every post as though they were expecting some sort of aggravation or assault from the caged men. I glanced around only to see the male security stood stiff as board dutifully. There was nothing done or say in sometime past more than the mumbling from the returnees. Although I did not hear the call about the liaison officer arriving the men seem to be well informed about this would be taken place soon.

282.   Even those who were asleep soon were tumbling from it and I could hear the sliding door movement. The men coming out to pay attention to what was developing right there and then about what would be said and for their reassurance of when their flight would be. Flymug suggests and claim that those who were asleep do so because they avoid eating and so reduce their spending and starve the airport out of capital income. Harriett stood by me and the other man and so was Flymug as we waited and looking upward about what the men on top of the stairs about to tell us. Not knowing the other man's name I ask to see had Harriett knows it. He did and told me to call him, "Stinky."

283.   "Call him Stinky, he'll answer to it." Harriett laughingly said. "Yes. But don't call him Stinka, he

won't like that. Goes mad and you'll be in trouble. Good man he is." "Ever hear anything of Matthew?" I was hoping that Harriett might know something up to date about Matthew. But the discussion were cut short when attention were called by a man stood on the stairs and officers approach too and stood instead on the balcony above the man that called attention from load haler. I keep glancing around to see the crowds of men gathered. They seem were creeping out of every holes and corners of the building forming a huge streams of men coming and almost to the point to blocked the huge walk ways.

284.   Seem like months they were packing peoples into this building and if I had seen half these men at Leesburg when first I travel to the south it would reduce my fear. It would be a softener to take in the hugeness sea of the crowds of men gathered and pressing against one another having nowhere else to stand except where their feet space were, and looking upwards to the gods. There they were on the top of the balcony waiting for the men to subdue to them in silence, and until they were, they looking down at us without saying anything. The chatterbox continue to irritate the charged situation and for a time the liaison officer with his team may wanted to call off the instruction he wanted to deliver to those men who were chattering including those that were not.

285.   Then it went so far as when the man with the load hailer continued retake the silence illicitly, but it was hard to keep abreast of the mumbling sound that

continue to disrupted the instruction that were to be given. At least it was raining but hot in summertime in Florida just gone mid afternoon. Those in the far distant may hear only the sound of the load hailer but not to what was being said although it seem that they have turn the volume up it was vibrating out the spoken words that came out muffling. Those who herd and understand what was said would pass it down to the others who probably because of mumbling did not hear so well what was being said, and even though I was close to the speaker still I was having trouble understanding what the speaker was saying.

286.   Some of what was said clearly would have to internally interpret and I keep a keen lookout about things that would be going on around about, at that time hoping that my name would be called with my McDonald number for clarification. This was a sort of national insurance number that we were given during our travel. The airplane was on the tarmac waiting for those whose name was called to load the liaison officer hailed. Many of those names called we would not see them again throughout this life time and neither would they either. It appears that what Mr Jiles was telling us at the mechanical school sometime ago revealed to me that he was right all along although I have had no reason to disprove or doubt what he was telling.

- CHAPTER -
TWENTY SIX

287.   I remember many instances where other trainees who would by now passes out and become indentured would be joking about the exact experience that I am now experiencing. On this point I remind myself that sometimes in the future I would be telling about my first travel too, and might be laughed at as much by younger or other juveniles and even by adults who had never travel. Upon learning that most if not all of us would be on our way home during that evening I was hopeful. The meeting with the travellers were not as smooth as the authorities might have like. But it seems that they understand that with so many men gathered total silence would be unobtainable. Although they tried to stamp some authority on the overall meeting it would not work solely for that purpose of unwillingness by the men for silence.

288.   After the continued misbehaviour even at the point of threatening to call off the meeting some were still being argumentative. Those who want to hear but could not do so without several rebuking by their friends to stop the chattering with interference with the men giving out the information to us. At this point many had things to say but it was too late at this time to deal with. They did not have time from both sides to deal with past issues that should have been raised and dealt with many months or even years ago. But for me, it was another feature of travelling with the older men who seem careless of their views how it might have been interpret following their viewpoints raised. Some

of them were very angry about certain behaviour of the authorities regarding farmer workers treatment for some reason or the other.

289.   But none of their grieve were going to be dealt with now and even their views would be suppressed even if they were reasonable at the moment and would have no relevant benefit, unless it was going to be incorporated for the next time in the farm workers charter, if there was any. There were no noticeable people taking notes of any suggestion made regarding anything the men said or were heated up about. And so it was consider by myself the long drawn out interference was time waster, although we were wasting time, having nowhere else to go and was bound to listen whether it was in my interest or not. There was a cloud of resentment as the men barked, groan and staggered from one subject to the other without control of who they were that were listening. For those of us who interested in hearing what was being said have little way of calming the blistering groaning coming from disgruntle men?

290.   Ankle who wonderingly through the crowds came and stood by me looking up at the men that stood on the stairs. The man with the loud hailer came down and stood between the angry crowd trying to get something going or at least to calm it down so that the meeting could go on quickly. It seem that I was going back to the already experience and forward looking and saying that 'if the aircraft delayed for any reason that were caused by us-would they demand money from us

who were not the cause of the delay and go to those who were directly involved?' from Ankle, and Flymug, and the others who had travelled indicated before it was the normal aggravation. For this was mild considering many other instant.

291.   "Yes." Flymug asserted. "Sometime they have big punch up in here. Sometime their grievances didn't sort out and they come here thinking they'll do it here, before they board the plane." "It's pure drama." Henderson who came along too and quips. While the names were being called out to get their belongings and to follow the attendant that would walk those whose names were called out to the aircraft. The names were called out alphabetically and since I would be in the (P) I was away down the line to be called if I was going on this flight. Although being at the front because we had not moved since we came in set down beside our cases. The place was still damp even it was now a late sunny evening shines outside as the men dragged and pull their cases and baggage's for the loader to take them to the standing aircraft that remains hidden beyond the perimeter some distant away.

292.   Ankle was called in the first round, and then Harriett and Henderson followed closely behind. When Ankle name was called out he mention, "fought, boy, see you at Half-way-Tree a month time." That was how he bids farewell. I then taken him up and ask him what that was for. "That's the time McDonald sends your savings down. Don't you want it?" He asked as though

he expected me to refuse it and reply 'no.' But I reply and say 'yes.' "See you there then." They said to me. I looked out to the long line of crowded men that form a worm like line curvature bend around and going on and becoming smaller and smaller as the distant divided between them and me. "How many men women and children have I seen during my travel?" I pondered. "A thousand-more-quarter of a million, maybe, maybe more-including those that I meet regularly. Those passes by and those I saw from a distant just as I was now looking on these men who soon disappear into the nothingness of time. Those that I have seen and didn't count were now the same as those gone along in this immediate crowd."

293.   There were men whose name still being called out. Even the buses now came along that would take them to an aircraft and the smaller vehicle that was loading on the luggage. Those men in the long line were carrying their personnel belongings on their backs with little packages holding done at hand length while their heavier belongings they left behind for vehicle that would carry them out to their waiting departure plane. Dramatising the scene for me would continue as long as I live as part of a life event. Soon too I would be on that march as well never to return the same. Probably some others would looking out for me, whether I would be walking out too from their vantage point to see whether I was in the front, middle or at the rear the last or when I would disappear in the long line of nothingness.

294.   It was late in the evening when the men in suit return of that same day and although there were considerable amount that had gone home the base was still crowded as though the amount was not reduce. There was no provision for official meal to be served. Those who knew the running's brought biscuits and smaller package that they would share with their friends and colleagues, and probably give a stranger a biscuit or two if he sat nearby and looking on as a dog looked to every pinch the master puts into his own mouth. Page collected a hundred and seventeen dollars and fifty cent from the suit he sold to Britain and beside the updated pay packet from the owner. Added to the reduce pile I had left over from the north that runs into a few hundred dollars I was taking back home.

295.   But I could not afford to spend any of those dollars considering the exchange rates worth against sterling which I did not know, but surmise the dollar value would be less than half in the sterling worth. I stuck my two hands into the back packets of the jean I wore moving slowly around my case and listening to the oratory given by the men in suits who were standing on the stairs. Then I projected myself into the future dimension of the present even though I could not see it, it was there besides me for every footsteps I made. My name was then called out with instruction was to get my belongings out to the doors and follow the direction given by the security. By then it was getting dark and lighted up with official lighting that could be seen

distant away across and over some part of the airport perimeter. Aircraft were taking off and could hear the roaring as they took their hold in the skies. Some of them could for a short while be seen hurtling into the distant clouds.

296. The buses came along that would take us to our aircraft waiting to be loaded with farm workers going home. But before we could get onto the buses our photos were shown to each one with our name and number printed across the picture in three dimensional sensitivity projections. I became conscious of the time and turn my wrist to have a peek on what the time was reading on the seventeen jewel bullover with its Swiss movement reading. It tells seven thirty in the evening. Although it becomes darken on the ground there were still fiery skies to be seen far out into the distant heavens. The sun has not completely gone out of observation over the Florida skies. Had the aircraft was loaded with the farm worker and took of two hours time I would be back into Jamaica Palisados airport. There too it would be darken as well since both countries are in the same time zone.

297. Not long after we were going out onto the tarmac to the aircraft. It was a four engine propellers plane. Whose blades droop down and stood like a crow in the night with its long and slender body waiting to take us off into our oblivious future. I followed the group that was going and leading the way on entering into the aircraft I could hear some sound calling. "Page,

Page, you son of gun!" I recognised the voice that of Descaster, but I could not turn around to acknowledge as I being pushed forward by the men behind to push those in front of me. Then I was shown to my seat and for awhile I sat and watch those men who were following after me pushes their way forward up the aircraft aisle.

– CHAPTER –
TWENTY SEVEN

298.   Soon the flow of men stop coming and only a trickle passes by. In the seats there food packs accommodatingly placed on them. Then instruction were given regarding seats belt and safety, I could hear the engine and also feel the vibrating and soon it was moving followed by excessive noise as it lifts an soon we were in the dark sky over Florida glades. I then know for certain that I was on my way home the man sat beside me commence to eat from his pack and I commence to follow him to eat too. He did not show any dread and it seems that he was well travelled and was comfortable more about his food than anything else.

299.   It was just after eleven 'o' Clock when the plane landed and shortly we were walking off to collect our belongings. Since it was my first travel I would hesitate to go forward because I considered to make a wrong move may ender or jeopardise the timid flow. So then I was told what and what not to do. Before I collect my trunk from the revolving belt when Descaster a good old timer came and catches up with me. "Back on the rock, boy." He murmured and sounds as if he was disappointed to me. "I left here a juvenile and return a juvenile, what change?" I jested. "Any regrets?" "Yea. I make some good friends in my journey and lost them before I return. Ended up back to whcrc I started. I came back more confused, I tell you than before." I replied. "Didn't want to come back, I see?" "O yea, wants to come back alright, but before I go away I got people responsible for my out going, but now I don't

know where to start." "Grow up!" Descaster Barked while I was lifting the trunk off the belt and that was where we left it only to say our farewell when a taxi came and sped him off to his home.

300.   I stood outside after they let me through the custom not listening to the garbling noise but my night was taken to ask- where will I go and lay my head until the daylight? The tumbling rocket to where would I be tomorrow or some other time from this instant. My mother and guardian lived in the country and for certain she would be glad to see me return. My guardian might too, but they may consider that I gave up a good career to put myself on unaffordable life style which I would not able to maintain for adulthood and that of a family. My mother tells us that whenever we were in doubts to pray and she pointed out that we might even go further, 'kneeling on your knees and do so to your heavenly father.' This we never missed out on of her offspring. When I do this it never fail to get some sort of result in my favour. So I took a little time out and stood leaning against the column holding onto the handle of the trunk and put a petition in for him to consider me now.

301.   It was not long before I made up my mind to go and see my guardian, and prepare to meet the consequence, good or bad. Then at once I acted upon the thought and hail a taxi that would get me to the country home in St Catherine and gave the driver the address. Many of the roads were blocked through heavy rain and cause flooding and almost delay my anxious

anxiety which I need to explain to my guardian with exceptional apology straight away. But it could not be if the transport was flying it was not immediate enough. Anyway when we got there it was well passes midnight and gone over into the next day but assuming that by now they were well asleep snugly.

302.   When the taxi pulled up at the gate at my guardian home, I lost my nerve and ask the taxi driver to knock on the door for me. Soon the whole neighbourhood woken up and before I could greet my guardian and his wife properly people were already coming to see the traveller return from his distant travel. The family receive me as though I was important to their whole living and although it suppose in my mind that I owed an apology immediately, they lighted up the whole house by their wholesome laughter and touching and hugging and haughty with excitement. I consider it would be inconsiderate for the due apology to happen immediate although knowing that it will be due in the near future. No sooner my bed was made and all it needs was a carcase to lie in it comfortably. I slept comfortable until the daybreak in the afternoon when my mother came in the room to take a peek at me sleeping.

303.   She too was exited and hugged me motherly. Thereupon I came to realise that in the inner mind there was something there that can be freighting and led to timidity. Soon after the excitement I then wanted to see my girl Julie Rose and visit the mechanical school and to see also Mr C Jiles at the same time but afterwards.

Might be, late by the time I caught another taxi vehicle into town, but I could not wait for next day and my eagerness was driving my mood. Since she would not know that I came home and was now on the island. My guardian and his wife were talking about me that was observable passing glances across the room with my mother as well. They were talking in signs and agreeing which older people understand not knowing that I was observing their discretely tell tale action. It was not long before my guardian said, "If you're going in town and going to look up Jiles you won't find anybody there." "What you mean?" I asked thinking that Mr Jiles had died.

304.　"They raided his place and found he was doing license so he's in jail, a week ago now. Its several point they raided. Island wide raid and all the big men are in jail." He explained. "What happen to the apprentices?" "Some of them were in the fraud as much." He replied. "You too probably would be in it. We were glad knowing that you weren't there." "I still have over a year to go." I replied. "You can make up for it now you might want to go to England. Your bones aren't started to creek yet." He said. "That I'll do after I married Julie Rose." I replied. "I have enough I think to do all of that." "No!" My guardian replied. "There's some money about for you. You may want to consider using up some of it." "Thanks." I inserted and looked at my guardian and still ponder whether, if I had not sold my first suit it could fit my guardian and make a wonderful present with

the blessing of UNCLESAM. "What's in the heart of a Juvenile?" I pondered and Conclude.

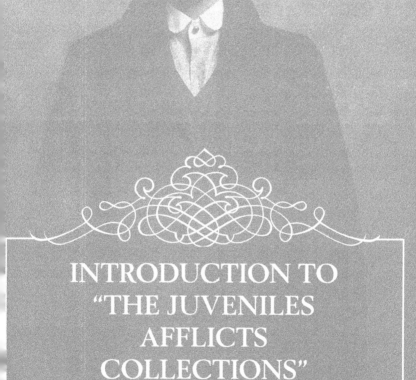

INTRODUCTION TO "THE JUVENILES AFFLICTS COLLECTIONS"

Page [Pcagd] Taken Himself Out Of His Parental Care To Travle To The United State Of America. The Offer Was For Once In A Life Time And He Had To Quickly Make The Choice To Go Or Not To Go. He Was Scared To Make This Break Away And Worrried About The Backlash If He Fails. However, Some Elders On This Travel Comes To His Rescue, But He Still Feeds On His Reflection And Reminised Often On His Young History. He Was Faced With Many Attemps To Failure Which Stared Him In His Face At Time. His Handling Of Attemps And Others Were Grooming Him For The Future, And Comforted Himself Throughout His Constant Reflection On Past History In This Juvenile Short Life Lived.

305. The young juvenile make a decision whether he wanted to be an indenture motor mechanic with an open cheque for jobs or exchange it to go and work on the farm in United States of America, where he could gets more money. Albeit the overseer told him of the consequences, but then offered him his blessing while he was discussing the problems he had. Earlier on in his travel he finds things very complex and unbalance but now that he had make his first decision he got was to stick with it and learn from experience.

He forms alliance with this older traveller that shows and tells him about contract workers. But this traveller he learns that he was a communist in the meantime although he did not know what communist was about. He was growing up in a grown up world where things have its good points and bad points. This story included dramatic events going on his fate the Page story of the Juveniles Afflicts Collection. (PCAGD)

Page was growing up, sticking to his mother and others experience input but his mind and soul were spiralling out of focus and activated like volcano eruption. Within his body, there was something planted that he could not tell or describe and had to resort and conclude that it must be the way it is when becoming an adults male.

The older women hardly tell their boys about growing up and very seldom do about the opposite sex and sexual attraction. Many boys and girls come to grief at an early age because parents consider that the little girl or little boy unable to attracted to their opposite so early. Young men will barrow from their pairs, but the older man who interested in younger men will tell facts about the big world that would not have discover elsewhere or until trouble start.

Matthew was this kind of an older man and forms in Pages mind a role module, he often reflected on. He become on sailable adults, although their time together was short. It fills Page's needs and was right at the right time as to the quote from an unknown poet that: "In the heart of a seed buried deep so deep. Dear little plant lay fast asleep. Awake! Said, the sunshine, and come out

to the light. And the little plant heard and it roused to see what a wonderful host this world may be."

PS: NAMES HAVE BEEN CHANGE TO SUITABLE CHARACATERS-THE END.

Lightning Source UK Ltd.
Milton Keynes UK
UKHW010937280919
350633UK00001B/3/P

9 781728 394190